FEELING FRISKY

edited by David Laurents

PROWLER BOOKS

Feeling Frisky edited by David Laurents

First printing July 1999. Printed in Finland by Werner Soderstrom Oy.
Cover photography by Glenn Studio © 1999 Prowler Press

web-site: prowler.co.uk
• ISBN 1-902644-15-8

British Library Cataloguing in Publication Data.
A catalogue record for this book is available from the British Library.

<u>CONTENTS</u>

AFTER HOURS
by Chris Leslie

The best part about night life in New York City is that the game is not over when you leave the club. If you don't find someone while you're out, there are plenty of good-looking guys on the street. At closing time, certain neighborhoods are crawling with guys.

One night when I was out late I decided to cruise the neighborhood a little before heading home. I walked over to Ninth Avenue and started walking uptown, checking out the surprising number of drunk Chelsea boys walking their dogs and partaking in otherwise suspicious activities. I reached Twenty-Second Street and headed east, intending to hop on the F train and head home.

Fortunately, I was waylaid. About halfway down the block, this rather short but wide man passed me. He was kind of cute, so I looked back over my shoulder a few steps after we passed. He was looking, back, too. I took a few more steps and looked back again, and again he was looking at me. I stopped walking and turned around, trying not to look too threatening. He looked back a few more times but didn't stop walking, so I started to follow him.

When he got to the park on the corner he jumped the fence and disappeared into the bushes. I followed, and found him standing against a tree. Without a word, he unzipped his navy blue parka and put his hand on his crotch. I stood in front of him and nodded my head. He nodded back, looking me in the eye, and unzipped his pants. He looked a little fat at first, but as he opened his coat I realized that it was in fact the layers of clothing that made him look so bulky. He was shorter than me with longish brown hair that was thinning a little over his temples. He was wearing a white T-shirt and black jeans, and a baseball cap that advertised a brand of farm equipment.

He pulled out his dick and I followed suit. It was pretty cold out, and his dick was shriveled up to an embarrassing size. I was a little hornier, but even so my half-hard dick recoiled at the cold air. I took a step closer to him and grabbed his dick away from him. Jerking us both off, I started to get harder but his dick remained flaccid. I began to get nervous -- this park, now closed for construction, used to be a popular cruising area until a few gay-bashings occurred. I wondered what he was up to -- he looked gay, certainly, but you never know these days.

"Do you want to suck my dick?" he asked, roughly. I looked around to make sure that there was no one there and squatted down. I put his flaccid dick into my mouth and started to suck. He started muttering all the standard shit -- "Yeah, suck that cock" -- while holding my head with strong hands. I reached up and felt his stomach, and instead of a paunch I found carefully sculptured abs. His thighs were thick and beefy. Despite myself, I started to get turned on by his huge, muscular body.

But for whatever reason, his dick refused to get hard. I jerked off while sucking him. When I started to get really turned on, though, he pulled me off his dick. "This is no good here, guy. Do you want to come to my place?"

"All right." I said. I stood up and we put out shit away. I followed him out the park, and we walked to his apartment a few blocks away. We didn't talk much; we exchanged names and trivial information. He told me he was born in Pennsylvania, he had just moved to the city about two months ago, and he was twenty nine. He wouldn't tell me where he worked ("mostly odd jobs").

He lived in a standard city brownstone. His apartment was on the top floor, and we had to climb five flights of stairs. Once inside, I took of my coat and sweat shirt. He got himself a beer and went into the bathroom. I sat down on the couch to look at the bookshelf, trying to get a clue as to what this guy was all about. There was a lot of weird titles there -- shit like anthologies of essays on Jacques Lacan, books by Michel

Foucault, and other pop postmodern study aids. While it was stuff that no casual reader comes across, the collection lacked any quirks -- science fiction novels, or biographies, or murder mysteries -- that would indicate some kind of intellectual personality.

When he got out of the bathroom, I nodded to the bookshelf. "So, do you go to school?"

"No," he said. He saw me checking out the bookshelf and added, "those are my roommates' books. He's into some pretty heavy stuff."

"So where does your 'roommate' sleep?" I asked.

He ignored my question. "You want to suck my dick?" he asked. He sauntered over to the couch, unzipping his pants as he walked. Standing in front of me, he pulled out his soft, small dick. I took it into my mouth, and did my best to suck on the limp meat.

"You better be a good cock-sucker, guy. I've been doing coke all night."

That would explain it. I reached inside his fly and pulled out his balls, which were freshly shaved. Massaging them with one hand, I sucked hard on his cock, trying to break through his coke haze. His dick got a little bigger -- but he didn't really start to get hard until I started to moan a little, like the idea of sucking his dick was turning me on. That works every time, and his dick started to swell as I pretended that I liked nothing better to suck on some Chelsea boy's flaccid dick. I rubbed his thighs, which were also shaved, and then moved around to his full, hard ass. He was quite built, by far the largest boy I had ever had sex with, and the novelty of it all started to turn me on in spite of myself.

The boy started to moan, and his dick continued to grow. To my surprise, it was getting really long and thick -- I wondered how far it would go. I picked up the pace, moaning and breathing heavy, and soon he clasped his hands behind and started to fuck my face. He started to moan, too, and as his dick grew to choking size, it still wasn't really hard. Cool.

"I'm gonna fuck you so hard, boy. I'm gonna fuck you with this dick so hard that you're gonna cry," he muttered. With that, his splincters contracted, and a little pre-cum leaked out. He was really getting himself turned on. Suddenly, he pulled out and stood back. "Take off your clothes," he said. I unlaced my boots and pulled them off, then stood and stripped off my shirt and pants. My dick wagged out of the my boxer's fly. I grabbed it and started to jerk off. "All of them. I want you completely naked." I pulled off my socks and underwear. "Go into my bedroom and wait for me," he said.

I walked down a short hallway. Past the bathroom there was a door which I expected was his bedroom. I opened the door and was greeted by a rush of cold air. Once my eyes adjusted to the low light, I saw all sorts of dirty clothes littering the floor and draped from the loft bed. After looking about, I climbed up to the loft.

A minute later the boy joined me, condom and lube in hand. I lay on my back, and he rubbed my thighs and chest for a minute. "You've got a hot body," he said. He grabbed my dick and jerked me off a little. I closed my eyes and threw my hands over my head, expecting at least a little service. All he gave me, though, was a quick little suck before he remembered the role he was playing. He got up on his knees and ripped open the condom. "I can't wait to fuck that ass."

He unrolled the condom, but his dick had softened to a point where he couldn't get it on. "Come here and give me a hand. I'm still a little high." I got up and he pulled my head to his crotch. "Get that dick ready for your ass," he said.

Within seconds he was fully hard again, this time much bigger than I had remembered. "Get that rubber on my dick," he said. I unrolled the condom over his dick, then covered it with lube. It was actually quite big, and I conserved a little lube which I discreetly applied to my ass hole as I got on my back. He lifted my legs into the air. "I hope you're ready, boy." he said. "This is going to hurt." I doubted it, but I kept my mouth shut as he leaned forward and pushed into me with a firm pressure. Once he got it home, he pulled my ankles to his chest.

Big, white boys from Chelsea certainly are not my thing. But since I was here, I planned to take full advantage of the situation. I moaned and muttered incoherently. And then I started to feel his huge shoulders and tight waist, and as my moaning and touching turned him on, he started to fuck me harder and deeper. And in spite of myself, I started to get turned on, too. I sincerely started to moan, and muttered for him to fuck me.

He could tell the difference, and as I started to really get into it, he started to play it up a little. "Yeah, you like my dick, don't you?" he asked, slapping my ass. I moaned back, and reached down to start jerking off. "Don't touch your dick, fag. I'm gonna fuck you so good that you won't need to jerk off." I put my hands back on his arms again, which were so fucking muscular and tight.

He closed his eyes and held my ankles tightly, releasing them only to slap my ass, hard, from time to time. "You fucking whore. You just walk the streets, waiting for someone to fuck you. You like being a whore, don't you?" He slapped me hard on the ass and jammed his dick deep inside my ass. I winced in pain, and turned my head away. "How much are you gonna charge me for this?" He was ramming me hard, and starting to get out of breath. "You should pay me, faggot. I'm giving you what you need."

I started to get a little nervous, and must have tensed up because he calmed down a little. He slackened his pace and stopped going so deep, getting my ass back in the mood for his dick. "You're so hot," he whispered a few times, uncharacteristically tender. The boy was pretty high, and he kept things going at the same pace, like a machine, for longer than I thought I could take it. Sweat was dripping off his brow, stinging my eyes, and everywhere our bodies touched was slick.

Finally, the repetition sunk through his coke haze and he started to get closer to cumming. His dick started to expand as he entered the home stretch. He opened his eyes and kissed me as he pushed my thighs up against my chest, holding my ankles nearly at the level of the bed. I could hardly breathe, but the position opened my ass up wide, helping to accommodate his growing shaft. "This is how I fuck my girlfriend," he whispered. He started to grunt, and fucked me with short, hard thrusts. I was boiling inside, and finally he told me he wanted me to cum for him. He put my hand on my dick, and commanded me to shoot while I fucked him. Within seconds, I was shooting a load that I won't soon forget as my ass clenched tight around his cock.

After I finished cumming I tried to get him to pull out, but he would have none of it. "Give me what I paid for, you fucking whore," he said. "You came too fast, now you're gonna pay." He forced my knees into my chest and eased his dick deep inside my ass. I squirmed and tried to get him off, but he held me still. I'm sure he would have given up if I put up a serious struggle, but I decided to lay still for a minute, waiting for him to cum, before realizing that my struggling was turning him on. I started to struggle again, and muttering things like his dick was too big and that I couldn't take it. Within thirty seconds his dick was throbbing cum into the condom inside my ass.

After cumming, he collapsed onto me for a minute, out of breath. "That was really good," he said after a moment. He leaned over to kiss me, but then we heard the door slam. We looked over, and his boyfriend was just coming into the apartment. I thought it was an amazing coincidence until I realized that he must have entered the apartment in the middle of our fucking, watched most of the show, and then slammed the door afterward so that we would know that he came in.

The boy leaned down to kiss me again, and I asked him if I should take off. He said not to worry about it. "Isn't that your boyfriend?"

"Yeah," he said. "But don't feel like you have to rush off if you don't want to." He kissed me, then jumped off the loft and went to the front of the apartment. I lay in his bed as he had a whispered conversation with his boyfriend. I lay glowing for a few minutes, and then peeked out the bedroom door, trying not to get lube or butt juice on the sheets, which seemed like they had just been washed. I could see my boy's cute ass and shoulders, and that was about it. I laid back down and waited for him to finish chatting with his boyfriend.

It seemed like they were going to talk forever; maybe they were in the middle of an argument. I got off the loft and walked into the bathroom. They were quiet when I came out of the bedroom, but started talking again once I closed the door. I wiped the lube and juice off my ass with some toilet paper, washed my face, and ran some water through my hair (it was cropped really short, but still was sticking up in a weird way).

I came out of the bathroom in time to be introduced to the boy's boyfriend before he walked into the bedroom. I looked at the boy and shrugged my shoulders. He came over, put his hand on the back of my head, and kissed me. We kissed, dry, for a minute, and then I said I should be going. I dressed quickly as the boy washed up in the bathroom. He showed me to the door, and he kissed me again before I went down the stairs.

NINE LIVES
by Dominic Santi

So I can lick my own dick now. I don't like the taste of fur. Reincarnation is not all it's cracked up to be.

I lowered my leg and stretched, kneading my claws in the Irish linen tablecloth. I've always liked the finer things in life. Not that I was supposed to be playing centerpiece. But Steve had outdone himself this evening. The table was set for a seduction -- good china, Waterford, sterling. Jarre playing softly on the stereo. Candles. I was trying to be helpful.

That cute little trick he'd picked up on Santa Monica Boulevard last night was definitely worth the effort. At least, I assumed he would clean up well. The Halloween costume had covered too many of his assets for my taste, but a basket like that is hard to hide. And I know there were nipple rings hidden under that Roman soldier's tunic.

I never would have bought the guy's "not tonight -- I'm drunk, and I want the first night with you to be special" routine. Granted, he and Steve had seemed to have more than a passing interest in each other. But I was a real slut in my previous life. I would have wanted that little snuggle bunny drunk and sober.

I nuzzled the rim of a wine glass, marking it with my scent. That was a close as I came to a man's lips these days. All I got to do was watch. Well, almost all. I sat back down and raised my leg again, giving myself a couple of quick licks. There were some compensations.

Doorbell! I hopped down off the table and ran under the loveseat, peeking out as Steve opened the door.

Oh, yeah. Even without the costume, this one was a keeper. Not too tall. Gymnast's build. Soft brown curls and hazel eyes. And dimples! Quite a contrast to the former middle weight wrestler with the close-cropped blond hair and green eyes that I'm used to seeing crawl out of bed each morning.

Our guest blushed as he handed Steve a bouquet of yellow roses. Half a dozen. Tastefully understated.

Steve was eloquent, as always. "Wow, you're even cuter than I thought! Um, . . . Mike?"

Smooth move, cowboy. I sighed and shook my head.

The date didn't do much better. "Thanks. You, too . . . Steve?"

Human intellect is vastly overrated. They'd gotten the names right, but it was definitely time to take matters into my own hands. I raised my tail and sauntered out into the entry.

"Meow." Not too loud. Polite. Inquisitive. Just enough to get their attention. As usual, it worked.

"Hey, that's a beautiful cat!"

Mike reached down to pet me and I gifted him with one more quick meow -- slightly friendly, appropriately regal -- as I rubbed up against his khaki pants.

"Dammit, Bagheera! You're getting fur on him!"

I sneered at Steve as he pushed me out of the way. The fur looked rather good, I thought. Short, black wisps all along the calf. A nice contrast to the cream of the fabric.

Steve stumbled all over himself with apologies. "Hey, man. I'm sorry. You want me to put him in the bathroom?"

Ha! Not without chain mail, you won't!

I was tempted to teach Steve a lesson. With company this good in the house, he knows I'm going to be a guest at the party. Steve took a step towards me. I growled, feeling the frisson all along my back as my fur rose.

Fortunately, Mike stepped in before Steve got hurt. "I really like cats. And this guy seems friendly."

If nothing else, Mike certainly knew how to make brownie points. I gave Steve a look, then pointedly ignored him as I marched back to rub against Mike's leg again. I smirked as Mike scratched behind my ears. Good technique. He knew right where the sweet spots were.

When I'd been petted enough, I turned and led the three of us into the living room for some hors-d'oeuvres and wine.

I stayed until I was comfortable they'd be able to handle the conversation on their own for a few minutes. I can never be too sure with Steve. Graphic designers are so unpredictable. But he seemed to be doing okay, and I was hungry. I figured I had time to grab a quick bite from my bowl before dinner. Besides, Steve wouldn't make any moves until after he'd served the entree. He'd spent hours on dinner, cooked the marinara sauce from scratch to impress this guy.

I walked into the kitchen and sat down. Kibbles. Oh, joy. But it was better than starving. I batted a couple onto the floor, then settled in and started crunching.

I don't know exactly how I got here. Got to be a cat, that is. One moment I was a human, waking up with this gorgeous, sated man in my arms. Having my way with him again anyway. Going out for breakfast together before I headed to the airport. Next thing I knew, I woke up in a pile of kittens.

Steve picked me out of the window in the pet store. At first, I wasn't sure how things would go. I approved of his reading material right off, especially the stroke mags on his nightstand. That first weekend, though, when he brought home a feisty redhead he'd picked up in a bar, I knew I'd found my home. I curled up on the headboard and watched them fuck each other senseless. Man, did that bedroom smell great.

Of course, I made Steve earn the privilege of my companionship. He takes care of me. I let him pet me when I'm in the mood. I purr when I want to. Nap. And we came to an understanding real quickly about this getting fixed business. I don't mark territory in the house. He ignores my propensity for extreme genital hygiene. And I get to watch him fuck.

Just thinking about that got my juices flowing. I finished my snack and went back into the living room to see how things were going.

The wine glasses were next to each other on the coffee table. Mike was sitting on the couch, leaning back into the cushions. Steve was on the other side of the room, perusing his music selection. They were talking about their jobs. Boring! But at least they were watching each other. Pretending they weren't. There was a nice little bulge growing in Mike's lap that he was trying to hide. It got bigger as Steve bent over to change the CD.

"What type of stuff do you have?" Mike stood up as he spoke, rearranging himself as he walked over to the stereo. He reached for Steve's butt, then stopped himself, pulling his hand back and wiping it nervously on his pants. His interest was tenting the front of his pants now, but Steve was facing the wrong way to notice. Mike waited, seemed to think about it for a moment, then leaned over Steve's shoulder, not quite touching, but way into Steve's personal space.

I felt like shaking the both of them. Steve's got a great ass! Reach out and grab that fucker!

"Do you have any more Jarre?"

Even I could see Steve's shiver as Mike's breath caressed his neck. Mike would have had to be blind not to see Steve's reaction.

"Sounds good. What else?" Steve popped the CD in and the two of them proceeded to fill up the carousel. Just standing there. Steve bending over the stereo. Mike bending over him. Both of them breathing faster. Their dicks hard. Almost but not quite touching each other.

I wanted to scream! That close, and they were tiptoeing around each other?!! Kiss him, you jerk! He wants it. He's waiting for it! Plant one right on his lips and shove your tongue down his throat!

I was halfway across the room, intent on bumping Mike's ankles, when he finally made his move. I shook my head and hopped up onto the easy chair instead.

Oh, okay, start out slow if you need to. Lick him. Taste him. That's it. More. Mmm, smell those pheromones -- somebody's dick is leaking. Now, arms around him. Nuzzle. You're getting it. Suck his lower lip. Harder. He likes it. Look at those hips wiggle. There's the tongue again. In. Oh, come on! I said IN! . . . Finally!

I turned around and draped myself over the arm of the chair. The old lion on a tree limb position. Nice firm pressure, my weight resting on my crotch as I rubbed back and forth over the padded upholstery, watching them really get into the kiss. It was a wet one, soft and greedy. Nervous. Exploring. Damn, what I wouldn't give to have lips again, and to have them that close to another man!

The ding of the kitchen timer barely registered with me, but Steve pulled back and smiled. "Dinner's ready."

Dinner? I couldn't believe it! Who gives a fuck about dinner?! You've got a hot, horny man in your arms!

My meow was loud and imperious, but the fools ignored me. Humans!

Steve took Mike's hand and squeezed it. "Want to help?"

"Sure." Mike planted a quick kiss on Steve's lips. They were was red and puffy, just waiting to be taken. Now!

Instead, Mike and Steve took hands like they were in some 1940's big screen romance, picked up their wine glasses, and walked into the kitchen, stopping every few feet to kiss again. Their eyes were glazed over. Both of them had wet spots where their cocks were bulging. I felt like banging my head on the chair.

I supposed it was easier for me to walk than it was for them. I didn't have clothes constraining my hard-on. But it was still damned annoying. And there's no such thing as resituating yourself when you have claws, retracted or not. I waited a few minutes, trying to calm down, then stomped around the corner into the kitchen. I really wanted to give somebody a good swift kick in the ass. A couple of somebodies!

Steve was slipping pasta into a pan of boiling water as Mike tossed the arugula into a vinaigrette. I hopped up on the counter and resigned myself to supervising. I used to be a big greens fan, but salads don't interest me much anymore. I was much more intrigued by the meat in those two baskets than I was in dinner. Steve wiped his hands on a towel, then opened the bag of rolls. He'd cheated and gotten those from the bakery.

"How do you like your buns?"

"Spread."

Not a good time for Steve to be taking another drink. I'm rather certain spewing wine onto his shirt was not the suavely dramatic effect he'd planned.

"Sorry, man." Mike laughed, pounding Steve on the back.

I shook my head. Choking on your wine. How gauche.

"You okay?"

The slaps slowed, and pretty soon Mike was rubbing Steve's back.

"I'm sorry." Mike was trying not to laugh. Almost succeeding. And blushing like a fiend. God, those dimples! "I shouldn't have said that. But . . ." If anything the flush got deeper. "Well, you do have a really nice ass." He reached down, tentatively running his fingertips over the edge of Steve's hip, kissing Steve's neck, waiting, like he was asking permission. "I'd really like to see more of it." He stopped, his smile fading as he looked up quickly at Steve's face. "But I can be versatile, too, if that's what you want. I mean . . ."

Those two were fawning all over each other like a couple of lovesick schoolboys! I gave Mike extra credit for keeping his hand on Steve's ass even as he stumbled around. But it was really starting to look like someone was going to have to drag those two into bed!

I wondered how Steve was going to react. He wants everybody to think he's mister butch top. But he loves getting fucked. He just won't do it unless he knows the guy well enough to be really comfortable with him.

Lo and behold, ol' Steve ate up that romance stuff hook, line, and sinker.

"I might like that -- you're being the top, I mean." This time it was Steverini with the red face. And he arched his tight, rounded butt right back into Mike's hand. Now, we were getting somewhere!

"Yeah?" Mike's arm flexed as he gripped the back of Steve's jeans.

Squeezing. Massaging.

Steve turned, moving all the way into Mike's arms, slipping his arms around Mike's waist. "Yeah."

This time, they were like anacondas. Tongues in each other's throats right from the start. Steve reached up between them, unbuttoning Mike's shirt. Fumbling. Then the fabric tore and buttons hit the floor.

Oh, yeah! Gold nipple rings! God, I miss nipples! Nuzzling around in a nest of fur, hunting for one to latch onto. Steve found what he was looking for right away. He took that pointed little titty in his mouth, and Mike went nuts.

I have to give Steve credit. He knows what to do with a good pair of nipples. He licked and sucked and chewed until Mike was backed right up against the counter, writhing and moaning, his hands buried in Steve's hair, holding him tight to his chest.

"Fuck, man. Fuck, that feels good!"

Damn, that kitchen smelled good. Man sweat and precome. There are advantages to having a sensitive nose. I could even smell the sauce burning.

Hello!

Now I heard it, too. Smoke rose from the uncovered pan, small flames flickering on the burner.

"MEOW!!!" I let out a certifiable feline screech!

They didn't hear the first one. Or the second. I had help with the third, when the smoke detector went off.

"SHIT!"

There was a flurry of movement as Steve yanked the pan onto an unused burner, turning off the stove as he flicked the fan on. Mike waved what was left of his shirt at the offending alarm until the godawful noise finally dissipated. They just stood there for a moment, looking at each other, surveying the mess.

Then they both burst out laughing.

"Damn. I really wanted to impress you." Steve wiped his eyes as he waved his hands at the ruins. "I spent all afternoon on that damned sauce."

Mike raised an eyebrow skeptically, then leaned his hip against the counter. "Too bad I didn't get to try it."

Ooh, these two were getting better. I sat back down on the counter. Steve spooned up a small cupful from the edge of the pan. Blew on the sauce until he seemed satisfied that it was cool enough. Then he stuck his finger in and lifted it to Mike's lips.

"Taste."

Mike licked the finger clean, sucking off every last drop. He kept sucking even when the sauce was gone. Their eyes were glazing again.

"It's good." He looked at the stove, then smiled as he kissed the tip of Steve's finger. "I think the noodles are overdone, though."

The noodles were mush. Mike and Steve both thought that was hilarious. Fortunately, Steve turned off that burner before the alarm started again. Then he took another fingerful of the sauce and spread it over Mike's nipples.

"These are still firm." He licked and sucked until Mike was moaning again. "And this."

Steve had bitched at me for getting fur on Mike's pants! His hand cupped the bulge in Mike's crotch, caressing, rubbing. Even I could see the stain spreading, and it wasn't all marinara sauce.

They didn't seem to care. The zipper whooshed. Steve shoved the pants and what had been pristine white briefs over Mike's hips. Scooped the rest of the cooled sauce into his hand and smeared it all over Mike's cock and balls. Then Steve dropped to his knees.

It was a good thing there'd been quite a bit of sauce left in that cup, because Mike was hung like a horse. There must have been 9 inches of marinara-covered sausage jutting up above those tight, furry balls.

I leaned back on the counter and threw my leg in the air. Now we were cooking!

Steve can really suck cock. He licked every drop of that sauce off.

Rolled Mike's balls in his mouth. Dragged his tongue up Mike's shaft one slow stroke at a time. Bathed that silky smooth skin until it glistened. Until the slit leaked pearls of precome. Then he opened his mouth and took the tip of that monster between his lips.

Watching that man give head is pure joy, and I was enjoying. Mike's groans were damn near as loud as the smoke detector had been. Steve started slow, working just the head, popping it in and out of his mouth, kissing it with the insides of his lips. Then he tipped his head back and opened his throat. He took that sucker all the way to the hilt in one thrust.

Mike yelled. I mean, like a scalded cat. But this didn't have anything to do with pain.

"Stop, man. Stop!" Mike pushed Steve back, hard, his hands shaking as he gasped for air.

"Didn't you like that?" Steve's voice purred like the cat who ate the cream, and I knew it was because he'd damn near gotten a throatful of it. "I only want to make you feel good." He gently kissed the tip of Mike's swollen dick.

Mike shuddered. I mean, his whole body shuddered.

"I want to fuck you. I mean it, Steve. I want to bury myself up your ass, and I want to do it NOW!"

Steve smirked, then his eyes got wider. It took me zero seconds to figure it out. Condoms and lube were in the bedroom!

Gym bag!

I damn near slipped on the linoleum as I leaped onto the floor and raced across to the shelf by the back door. Then I started furiously sharpening my claws on the canvas bag that held Steve's workout clothes.

He wheeled toward me. "Dammit, Bagheera! Stop clawing!"

Then Steve forgot about me as the light went on. He yanked the bag out from under me, unzipped the pouch, pulled out what he needed. A moment later, he was bent over the counter, his pants hanging off one ankle, his legs spread wide, wiggling his ass. I swear, that cute little pink pucker winked as it begged for Mike's attention. It didn't have to wait long. Mike shoved forward, hard and fast. Steve rose up on his toes, gasping as he cried out. But he kept his legs spread as he took that huge, latex-clad cock to the hilt on the first stroke, right up his wide-open, hungry asshole.

Mike thrust a couple of times, slowly, shuddering as his dick moved over that tightly stretched sphincter. Damn, that man looked hot. He even had dimples in his asscheeks! He grinned like a fool as Steve's hisses turned to mewls of pleasure. Then he started pounding into Steve. They went wild, yelling and writhing, slamming into each other, knocking things over. They fucked like lunatics! And they were way too horny for any kind of control. In no time flat, Steve shot all over the counter without even touching his dick. Mike was right behind him. He lifted Steve straight up off his feet, spread Steve's legs even wider, and buried himself up to his nuts in Steve's ass. That man came so hard the kitchen cabinets shook.

The room smelled heavenly. Like ass and come and hot man sex. I sat down on the floor, threw my leg in the air again, and, well, like I said, there are advantages to being able to lick your own dick. I indulged myself.

They ordered pizza afterwards. Ate it naked on the living room floor while they drank the rest of the wine. They were none too steady by the time they stumbled off to bed for dessert. But they'd been sober their first time.

And they shared the pepperoni with me.

LEASH BROKE
by Barry Alexander

Eating my silk shirt was the last straw. I signed Luther up for obedience classes the next day. I didn't even know why I was giving the stupid beast another chance. Technically, he wasn't even my dog. My lover had picked the overgrown monster out of a litter of cute little furry pups that some guy had in the back of his pick up. Almost purebred, he said. Purebred what, he didn't say.

Devon couldn't resist. Devon couldn't resist anything cute I'd soon discovered -- the car salesman, the new divisional manager, the pizza boy. By the time the cuddly teddy bear turned into a hundred pound behemoth with an insatiable appetite and no manners, Devon was history.

I was supposed to pick up some pizza on the way home from work, but I forgot. Devon ordered delivery. While we waited, Devon joked about all those ridiculous porn stories where the pizza boy really delivers. He stopped laughing when the guy brought our Canadian bacon and pineapple. He was cute. Devon couldn't resist. No, not right then, of course -- I was there after all. I should have suspected when I started noticing all the pizza boxes in the trash, but Devon could inhale pizza for breakfast.

When I came home early and saw Devon, draped over my kitchen table getting fucked by a naked guy wearing one of those stupid pizza-shaped caps, I knew it was time to end it gracefully. I screamed. I hollered. I whacked them with the pizza box. I knew Devon had cheated on me before. I'd been willing to put up with a few indiscretions -- Devon had a hard, gorgeous body and a hard, gorgeous, nine inch cock. What really pissed me off was that he'd had always told me he didn't like to get dicked. From the way he was moaning and groaning, I could tell how much he hated it. I'd never particularly wanted to fuck him, but that wasn't the point -- it was the principle of the thing.

While I was at work the next day, Devon moved out and took all of his stuff -- well, not quite all of his stuff -- he left me Luther.

I couldn't bring myself to take Luther to the shelter; it wasn't his fault. And he was kind of cute. He was a big, friendly slob of a dog with absolutely no manners -- and he was a better companion than Devon had ever been.

The dog trainer sounded very convincing on the phone. He had a firm, no nonsense kind of voice that sounded like just what Luther needed. When I pulled into the parking lot where the classes were held, I had second thoughts. It was total chaos: people milling, dogs barking, dogs lunging, dogs doing what dogs do.

I looked around for the guy with the sexy voice, but I didn't see him or anyone who looked like he was in charge. I spotted a little guy in a red dog club jacket leaning over and baby talking to a poufy little white dog. Maybe I should have fed Luther before I came to class. It was all I could do to keep him from dragging me over to eat the little Fluff-a-Poo.

"Ooh such a good puppy! Pretty baby! That's my girl!" the man crooned. You'd think even a dog would be embarrassed by that crap, but it was wagging its tail and following him around. Where in the hell was the real instructor? Then the guy gave the woman her dog back and walked over to me.

"Hi, my name's Jerry. I'm the instructor." He smiled and held out his hand, but I didn't dare let go of my leash. "Bill, right? We talked on the phone. And this has to be Luther."

"How can you tell?" What was this guy, psychic?

"Well, so far, he's the only dog that matches your description -- half-moose, I think you said. You look like you have your hands full. Why don't I hold him while you fill out the registration papers?"

I looked at the man doubtfully. He wasn't as small as I'd thought, maybe 5'7", but Luther was a damned big dog. I pictured him breaking away and swallowing Puff Ball in one gulp.

"He's pretty strong, maybe I should just put him in the car for a while." "Give me his leash," Jerry said firmly.

Even though I knew he'd never be able to hold Luther, I handed him the leash. No wonder dogs listened to him. There was no arguing with that tone. I hoped he had insurance.

"The collar's on backwards." Deftly, he removed the collar, flipped it over, and slid it back over Luther's head. "It's much easier to keep control when you have the collar on correctly." The collar looked exactly the same to me.

Just about then, Luther spotted the fuzz ball mincing past. I had a sudden vision of a screaming owner and a smiling Luther with a fluffy white tail dangling from his mouth. Before I could holler a warning, Luther lunged.

"Leave it," Jerry commanded as he turned and walked away. Luther never even got close to his intended snack. He hit the end of the lead, swung around, and found himself going in the same direction as Jerry. He looked as surprised as I felt.

Jerry reached down and patted Luther as soon as he was at his side. "Good boy," he said quietly, his voice deep and warm with affection. Luther wagged his butt, thumping Jerry's legs with his heavy tail. I felt like wagging my tail, too. Jerry's voice vibrated right down to my balls.

Impressed, I took a second look at Jerry. He wasn't bulging with muscle, but he had a nice solid build, maybe a little soft in the middle. His dark red hair looked silky, but it was standing up in clumps like he'd just run his fingers through it. He had light green eyes and a half-hearted attempt at a mustache. His skin was pale except for his sun-burned nose and left forearm. He wasn't great looking, but he was kind of cute and he had a wonderful voice. Not that I cared; I was looking for a dog trainer not a new boyfriend.

"The problem is he's not really leash broke. We'll work on that. Don't worry, with a little patience, practice, and praise, we'll soon have this fellow in line. And we'll work on your technique and timing."

I heard those three P's all through class. I got damned sick of them. I learned stuff I thought I knew: the right way to put on a collar, the right way to hold a leash, the right way to give gentle corrections. Jerry said to always use the same command, to speak in a firm confident tone, to give prompt corrections followed by praise. I needed to work on my voice, and consistency. I needed to teach Luther that I was the alpha male in our house. It all made sense, but it was damn hard remembering all of it.

Jerry demonstrated the proper techniques with his golden retriever. The dog marched beside him, executing turns and halts with military precision. The dog's eyes locked on Jerry's face and his tail beat back and forth like a metronome. He made it look so easy.

By the end of class, I was dripping sweat and my arms felt like they were going to fall off. We'd actually made it through the first class with no casualties. I felt terrific, then Jerry passed out the homework sheets.

He thumped Luther on the chest and gave him a dog treat. "You two are doing really well. In a week or two, you won't believe how much he'll learn. He'll even start to look forward to class."

"I don't know if I can last that long."

I didn't know about Luther, but I was starting to look forward to the next class. Jerry was terrific; he sympathized with my difficulties and always had a smile and an answer. He had a great sense of humor and he was so patient. He had to explain the same things over and over, but he never made me feel stupid. I liked that. I'm not the brightest guy in the world, but Devon had always acted like I was an idiot.

The second class went better, but I was still really getting a work out. Jerry and I chatted after class. Actually, he didn't have much choice. Luther pulled and drooled and whined until I let drag me over to Jerry. Luther was never one to forget a handout. "How do you manage with three dogs?" I asked Jerry. "I'm completely worn out. I never knew I was so out of shape."

Jerry eyes traveled down my body. Whoa! What was going on here? Was he checking me out?

"You look in pretty good shape to me. I thought maybe you worked out."

"Too much work, I do try to get in a little jogging every day."

"Perfect, take Luther along. Dogs love to jog, if you start them out easy. He'll keep you company and you'll burn up some of his extra energy."

Just when I started to wonder if he was interested, he turned the conversation back to dogs.

"He still pulls too hard. I wish there was someplace I could let him run safely."

"Well, I don't usually tell people this, but there's a small woods near my place where I take my dogs. There's no traffic, and no one ever goes there. Luther really gets along with my dogs. If you like, why don't you bring him out Saturday when I take my dogs out."

"Sounds great!"

We started taking our dogs out to run together. It was weird, I was seeing Jerry two or three times a week, but we weren't dating. It had been a long time since I had just hung out with another guy. I hadn't really considered Jerry as a potential lover, but the more time I spent with him the more I liked him. But how did I let him know I was interested without offending him in case he was some kind of homophobe? Luther was improving a lot and I didn't want to blow that.

I couldn't get a handle on Jerry. Was he always so friendly? He spent more time with me than any of the other students, but maybe he just thought Luther needed all the help he could get. Except for that one glance, he really never gave any indications of being gay. The couple of times I was at his house, I looked for signs -- Judy Garland posters, Bob and Rod coffee table book, rainbow pillows on a lavender sofa, leather jock straps under the cushions. Jerry had dog pictures on his wall, dog books on his coffee table, dog hairs on his gold couch, and leather dog leashes everywhere. Maybe he kept the leather jock straps in the bedroom.

I decided to test him. I left a copy of Harlan's Race on my dash and maneuvered him over to my car on the pretense of showing him Luther's new crate. He didn't notice. Maybe he didn't read much. I came to the next class with the windows down and a CD of show tunes playing at full blast. He didn't comment. Maybe he wasn't musical. So I wore tight jeans and a lavender tee shirt with a collage of tiny pink triangles. He didn't react. Maybe he was colorblind.

What did I have to do hit him over the head with my purse? Maybe he just wasn't interested. Was I even ready to deal with another lover? I wasn't that attracted to him. He wasn't really my type anyway.

But I couldn't stop wondering. I started thinking about Jerry when I jerked off. Was his hair really as silky as it looked? Did he have freckles everywhere? His big hands were so gentle with dogs; how would they feel on a man's body?

I had to know. The next Saturday I wore my "Hate is Not a Family Value" T-shirt, my lambda earring, and my tightest jeans. Before I went to the door, I put Luther out in the kennel with Jerry's dogs. I took a deep breath before I knocked. I might be losing the first new friend I'd made in a long time, but I had to know.

"Come on in," Jerry hollered. "I'll be just a minute."

I sat on the overstuffed couch and tried to choose the most seductive pose. Macho butch with legs sprawled open and arms draped across the back? Languidly, half-reclining like Marlene Dietrich? I tried several positions, but I still hadn't decided when Jerry came into the living room. He broke out in a big grin. For a moment, I thought he'd seen my contortions. I turned red before I realized he was reading my shirt.

"Are you trying to tell me something?" he asked.

"Yeah, I think the same thing you're telling me." I reached out and tugged the rainbow rings dangling from his neck as he sat down beside me.

"Hell, I've been trying to tell you for weeks. I thought you'd figure it out when I kept asking you over. Are you always this dense?"

"Well, you didn't notice my triangle shirt."

"Didn't you see the Pride magnets on my refrigerator? I even moved my Maplethorpe print into the bathroom so you'd be sure to see it."

"Hell, if you wanted to tell me why didn't you just leave a copy of Big Dicks in Tight Places on your VCR?"

"I was trying to be subtle."

"I was trying to be discrete."

"So now what?"

"Let's not talk about dogs tonight."

We looked at each other awkwardly for a moment, not sure what to do next. There suddenly didn't seem a whole lot to say. Maybe if we got out of his house for a while, I wouldn't be so tempted to just pounce on him and devour that dick I could see squirming around in his jeans. I didn't want to rush into this. Maybe a little kissing, a few harmless gropes before we moved on to the serious stuff.

"Why don't we go out and get something to eat? Luther's out playing with your dogs; he won't mind a late run."

"Great, how about pizza?" Jerry asked innocently.

"Pizza!" I couldn't help exploding. "I never want to see another damned pizza in my life!"

"Hey, it was just a question. What's the matter with pizza?"

So I told him. He started to laugh.

"I don't happen to think it's very funny."

"Come on, how many people do you know who got dumped for the pizza man. At least your boyfriend left you the dog. My ex ransacked my house while I was at a dog show. He'd have probably kidnapped my dogs if I hadn't had them with me. He took my CD player, my VCR, hell, he even took my dildo."

"Maybe he wanted a souvenir." I cracked up laughing. Jerry's sense of humor was contagious. It was funny now that I thought about it. We compared breakup stories. For the first time in weeks, I felt better.

"Yeah, well mine went back with his old boyfriend, the guy he said he wanted to see deep-fat-fried and served with mayo to a fleet of red-necked truck drivers," Jerry said.

"Devon would have liked that."

"Miles had delusions of gourmet cooking. He came up with the most inedible concoctions: chicken stuffed with apricots and anchovies in lime sauce, lemon-pepper liver with raspberry- glazed artichoke hearts."

"At least he tried, Devon never cooked. He thought pizza, Pepsi, and chocolate were the three major food groups.

"Men are the pits."

"Right!"

"We're better off without them."

"Right."

"You said it, girl!"

We sat for a moment looking at each other. Then we both just sort of leaned closer and kissed. The kiss was tentative at first, just a soft brushing of warm lips. We pulled back and looked at each other for a second. We were both breathing hard and I could see the desire in his eyes.

"We should take it slow," he said.

"Right," I agreed.

"There's no need to rush. Get to know each other a little."

"Right," I said. "No hurry at all."

We went for each other so fast we banged noses. I didn't care, I wanted to kiss him hard and I wanted to kiss him fast. I slanted my head and inhaled his lips, shoving my tongue rudely inside. His tongue flailed over mine in a liquid tangle of lingual pleasure. We fumbled at each other, hands diving under clothes eager to touch skin. His ring scraped along my chest as he tried to find my nipples.

"Do you ... want ... to go ... into the ... bedroom?" he gasped after he pulled his mouth away from mine.

"Too far away." I grabbed his head and pulled his mouth back to mine.

"Mmmyah," he mumbled around my tongue.

He got my shirt open and peeled it off my shoulders. He started to work my nipples, twisting and twirling the tiny knobs like he was trying to find the station on a cheap radio. It wasn't painful exactly, but it really didn't do much for me. I know some guys go really nuts over nipple play, but mine are about as sensitive as my knee caps.

He pulled his mouth away from mine and slurped a trail down to my chest. He really went at it, rasping his tongue over my nipples, sucking them into his mouth, blowing across the wet tips. I hated to see him wasting his time when there were so many other places that would really appreciate that enthusiasm, but I didn't want to hurt his feelings. Maybe he got off on it. Or maybe his old boyfriend liked it.

I was dying to have him use that warm mouth and tongue on my arm pits, but maybe he would think that was gross. Some guys did. Maybe if I just sort of nudged his head that way he would get the idea. Or maybe he would think I was just being pushy.

When I started to soften, I knew I had to say something. "Uh -- Jerry, you're doing a great job and everything, but uh, that really doesn't do much for me. I'm sorry, but I guess I'm just not too responsive there."

I was afraid he'd be offended but he just grinned at me. "No? OK, I'll just have to do a little exploring. How about here?"   H   e traced one finger slowly up my side. I shivered at the erotic sensation.

"Or how about here?" He trailed his tongue down my sternum and darted it into my navel. My cock jumped to attention. He stuck his hands in the back pockets of my jeans while he bent and licked and kissed my stomach. I could feel his warm hands cupping my ass through the denim. The pressure forced the jeans down exposing the top of my bush.

"What about this?" Jerry tucked his tongue under the waistband and licked down as far as he could. I groaned. If he didn't stop, I was going to cum right in my jeans.

I pulled him back up and kissed him, grinding my hard dick against his. His cock was so hard it could have qualified for a lethal weapon. I cupped my hand over his crotch and squeezed. "Finish the tour later, I've got to get a taste of this."

I pushed him back on the couch and knelt between his legs, struggling with his zipper. I swear the damn thing was rusty or something, I had a helluva time getting it open. He wasn't wearing any underwear. All that jostling and tugging must have gotten him really hot; his cock swung up and smacked me on the nose -- hard. That sounds sexy, but it stung.

The pain didn't slow me down. My eyes were still tearing when I caught his swaying dick in my fist. It wasn't really big but it had an interesting lilt to the left. I like cocks you can identify in the dark. It was thick and hard with a missile-shaped head. I liked the way he gasped and the little shudder that rippled through him when I swiped my tongue across the glans. When I pulled his jeans off, his balls plopped out and puddled on the cushions. The rosy orbs were lightly covered with red gold coils. I cradled them in my palm and swallowed his smooth pink dick.

He let me set the rhythm, making no effort to control my actions as I teased his cock with my lips and tongue, trying to see how much I could make him quiver. His big hands roved over my back, gently at first, but from the way his fingers started to clutch me, I knew I was getting to him.

Remembering how much he'd enjoyed playing with my nipples, I pushed his shirt up to expose his chest. His nipples were dark red against the cream of his skin and his chest was dotted with freckles. When I brushed my thumbs over the tiny points, he bucked against me so hard I almost gagged. As I worked on his cock, I repeated the motions he'd used on me and drove him nuts. He was getting so hot I knew I'd better cool things until I got him covered, besides my jaw was starting to ache.

Reluctantly, I let him slide out of my mouth. His cock was bloated and shiny with my spit. I dug into my jeans pocket for a condom, and spilled a handful on the floor. We must have had the same idea. Fumbling under the cushions, Jerry came up with a whole strip. He waved it like a banner.

"I was hoping we'd need more than one." he said.

As soon as we suited up, we squirmed around to feast on each other. Jerry was good at cocksucking. He didn't have any problem taking all seven inches of my aching dick. He knew how to keep his hands busy. He squirmed one big finger between my cheeks and played with my hole until I opened to him. His finger felt like a small cock as it wriggled inside me.

I copied his movements, just like we were still in class and he was the instructor. When my finger found his prostrate, he jumped, scraping my arm with his toenail. I jerked away and we both fell on the floor with a thud.

"What's so funny?" I asked when he started laughing.

"I guess it's true what they say -- love hurts."

We had a lot more room on the floor. We crawled all over each other exploring each other's bodies. I licked the fine red hairs on Jerry's thighs, slicking them down on his pale skin. When I moved up to lap his balls, he sighed and spread his legs. I cover his scrotum with tiny licks while he squirmed beneath me. He was really into it. He liked having his balls licked so much so that he came while I was trying to fit both of them in my mouth. His cum squirted into the clear tube like frosting in a pastry bag.

"It's been a while," Jerry apologized when his gasps subsided.

Simultaneous orgasms look great on film, but I prefer separate ones. I love that moment of total abandonment, when a man stops thinking and is totally caught up in the pleasure you've given him. If I'd known Jerry was so close, I would have watched. All I saw was the few square inches of flesh and sweaty pubic hair in my face and then it was over.

Devon would have rolled over and started snoring, the hell with whether I got off or not. Jerry didn't even wait to get his breath back before he started tonguing my body. This time I didn't feel any hesitation about guiding his head exactly where I wanted it. He did a great job on my pit, swirling his tongue around the wet hair and sucking in the damp flesh, then moving on to the other. He burrowed into the sweaty hollow as if he couldn't get enough. I stroked his silky red hair while he fed on me. He got me so hot, I had to have his mouth on my cock.

I checked to see if my dick was decent. I was still dressed for the occasion so I nudged his head south. He got the message. He swallowed my cock so fast it rammed the back of his throat. He gagged a little, but he didn't back off until he ran out of air.

He acted like he couldn't get enough of it. He worked his finger back inside my hole, making me grunt every time he bumped my prostrate. I reached down to jack his cock; he was already hard again. I slid the used rubber up and down his shaft, milking his cum down the sides. It smeared and spread over the latex until it look like transparent marble over his bright pink cock. It slid freely, like a juicy foreskin.

But I soon forgot Jerry's dick and concentrated on the hot mouth around my own cock and the thick digit exploring my rectum. When Jerry started pumping two fingers inside me, I couldn't hold back anymore. Neither could Jerry. He whipped off the used rubber and shot another load all over my leg. I locked his head to my groin and pumped that sleeve full of my hot juices.

Sex looks so effortless on videos. Everything fits together perfectly. No jabbing elbows, no pubic hairs caught between your teeth, no stubble burn. Everything is always perfect: the choreography, the timing, the setting. And I swear they must have a condom fairy on the set. Condoms magically appear and disappear at just the right moment. No deflated condoms oozing with chilled cum like the one dangling off my dick. There is no graceful way to get rid of a used rubber.

Jerry and I didn't fit together perfectly. His every touch didn't drive me to ecstasy. My nose hurt, my nipples were sore, and the cut on my leg stung. Sex with Jerry was sweaty and messy and wonderful. I wasn't in bed with some fantasy, air-brushed model. I was there with

Jerry -- love handles, uncut toenails, and all.   And he wanted to touch me, to give pleasure as well as take it. I felt the same way. I didn't know if I loved him, but I really liked him. Just thinking about doing it again was making me hard.

We lay on top of each other panting, our jeans still tangled around our ankles. Jerry was missing one shoe and I could see the hole where his big toe had poked through his sock. The sharpness of his sweat and the pungent odor of spilled cum filled the air. It was great.

"We should take the dogs out for their run."

"Right."

"We should probably cool off a little too."

"Right."

The dogs never did get their exercise that day, but we sure did. We even made it into the bedroom -- the third time.

SPANISH SUMMER
by Lawrence Schimel

I was sitting on a bench in the plaza below the street which led up the hill to the Alhambra when a man sat down next to me. It was a long climb to reach that red Moorish castle, and I wasn't yet ready for it. The walk across town had exhausted me, from the heat more than the exercise itself. The heat was why I'd come here: the Alhambra was the coolest place to be in Granada, because of the water gardens of the Generalife. The entire hill was covered with greenery, watered by the runoff from the countless fountains and pools.

I glanced over at the man who'd sat next to me, and realized he'd been staring at me. He met my gaze boldly and smiled at me, and suddenly I knew what was happening. I almost laughed. The heat had driven away almost all thoughts but finding someplace cool, and it had been so long since I'd been cruised--by a man, at least. Spain, and especially the small-ish town of Granada, was a culture which was so thoroughly based on heterosexuality--it even colored the language itself, with its masculine and feminine endings to words. The family I was staying with, and all my teachers and fellow students, were loudly homophobic, so I'd had to be very careful of what I said around them.

But now, it seemed, I'd stumbled across another gay man--or rather, I'd sat there and let him stumble across me. I looked around us, wondering if anyone else had noticed our brief interaction. I looked away from him, knowing I'd already decided to go home with him, or wherever--it had been so long since I'd felt another man's cock, my fingers itched to reach out for him, my mouth and ass yearned to take him in, even though he wasn't what I would normally find attractive. There was a hotel behind us, and as I thought about it, things suddenly fell into place--that this might be a queer cruising grounds. It was a place where many foreigners would pass through, almost everyone who came to the city made a pilgrimage to see at the Alhambra, and thus every gay tourist had to pass through it, too.

I was living here for part of the summer, so I didn't feel like that kind of a tourist. But I was playing a typical role in many ways. Europe seduces college students to come visit, with special tickets offering unlimited train travel and hostels at every step along the way, not to mention our own wanderlust. It's almost impossible to resist this siren call--no matter how tight your budget is, it's affordable--so I didn't put up a fight. The summer between my junior and senior year at college, I enrolled in a 6-week program through the University of Granada. I'd spend two months in Andalucía, surrounded by Spanish men, and then would spend the final month traveling, my SPARTACUS guide in hand, wherever my fancy took me.

That had been the plan. It was only when I got here that I realized it wasn't so easy finding Spanish men who were receptive to the idea of sleeping with other men, and hardly any who would identify themselves as gay. I knew there had to be more of a gay life that I simply wasn't finding, mostly because everyone I knew here was straight so I had no one to go with me in search of such nightlife. Occasionally I'd see flamboyant queens, the worst sterotypes of homosexuals--but I couldn't even cruise them or talk to them about where to go to meet men, since I only saw them when I was out with straights who I was afraid to let know that I, too, was gay. I knew I should stand up to my friends' and classmates' (and my own) homophobia and come out of the closet, but I was too afraid. Given the comments that they made about such outlandish and eccentric men, there was no way I was going to link myself to them in any way!

It was my first time traveling alone. I'd gone on trips with my family, around the States, and even to Europe twice before--Greece when I was thirteen, and England and Scotland when I was fifteen. But traveling on my own was going to be different. For months I had the most vivid dreams of various encounters I might have, with beautiful men, exotic and alluring, seducing me with liquid eyes and lilting accents, a mixture of romance and unadulterated carnal lust. We'd kiss at twilight in deserted parks, making out beneath overgrown statuary, and have sex in their apartments late into the night, then wake to sit all day in streetside cafés drinking and smoking.

I knew things wouldn't really go as smoothly, that these were all fantasies, the myth of Europe from movies and books, not the Europe I would really find. But I hadn't expected to feel so isolated, by my being gay more than by my being a stranger in a strange land. I was a foreigner to such rampant heterosexuality, and I longed for the comfortable gay sub-culture of college life, all of us full of young rage and rebellion, our support groups and monthly dances. My Spanish wasn't good enough for me to read the gay press--if there'd been any I could find, and I couldn't help realizing how lucky we had it back home in New York City, with three little weekly queer newspapers given out free on every street corner, and all the gay porn magazines that were available at nearly every magazine rack.

It had taken me days to find a kiosk in Granada which sold Spain's equivalent of gay pornography, and I then hesitated for two more days before going out late one afternoon with my backpack and walking clear to the other side of town to buy an issue. I didn't bother to flip through it as I might've if I were in the States--a little nervous, perhaps, at being seen by friends, but otherwise unconcerned. I thrust it into my pack and hurried away. I couldn't go home right away, but wandered all over Granada, pretending to sight-see, although I don't recall anything at all. Everywhere I looked I saw, superimposed, the scantily-clad cover-model.

As I roamed across the city, I wondered what the pages between would contain. I had a suspicion the magazine would be fairly vanilla: solo shots of men posturing in the nude, their hands far from their half-hard erections, lest they appear to be jerking off, and certainly nothing with another man in the scene. But right then, I was so desperate to see any cock, hard or soft, cut or uncut, I didn't care.

I sat down at a restaurant, even though I was so nervous at being discovered with a gay porn mag, and so anticipating getting a chance to actually read the magazine and jerk off, that I couldn't eat anything. but I wanted to use the bathroom, and that meant ordering something. "Churros y chocolate" I told the waiter, when he finally arrived. And, as he went off to bring the donuts and hot chocolate, I took my bag and went into the rest room, locking the door behind me.

Alone at last!

I sat down on the toilet and tore open my bag. The magazine was named MACHO, and I eagerly ripped off the plastic shrink wrap that prevented the curious from sneaking free peeks. I was hard before I even had the magazine open, my cock straining inside my jeans with the anticipation. I undid my fly with one hand as I flipped open the magazine in my lap. There before me was naked flesh: swarthy Mediterranean boys like I'd dreamed of, with long drooping cocks peeking out from dark folds of foreskin. I was shooting all across the pages in less than a minute, I'd been so worked up from the long weeks of fantasizing without any privacy or source of release.

I leafed through the entire magazine, memorizing every naked body, and left the magazine in the bathroom, afraid that it would be found by my host family when they cleaned my room. A bit expensive for a quick hand job, but worth every peseta. Those naked boys filled my fantasies and day dreams for many days to come.

But now, at last, I would have sex with another man again, not merely in my mind. I hardly knew the vocabulary to follow through on the pick up with the guy sitting next to me, but he understood that I would go with him. I tried to undress him, mentally, as we walked along streets that were half-familiar, but my mind kept going back to the image of the cover model from MACHO, the curve of his cock lifting up toward his navel, the dark ball sac hanging below, shrouded in wiry hairs.

The man I was following was in his mid-forties, I imagined, not unattractive, but not exactly my type, either. He was showing his age, thickening everywhere, although he sported muscles from a life of working manually. I wasn't proficient enough with the language to tell much about him by the way he spoke, just that he was Andalucían through and through and characteristically swallowed the ends of his words, making him even more difficult for me to understand.

But we managed to grope our way through the encounter. He tried for a pretense of civility when we got back to his apartment, but his heart wasn't in it as he offered me a drink and tried to make small talk: what we both wanted was to get it on already. He sat very close to me, and I could understand only every third word he said, so to shut him up and get things moving I finally leaned forward and kissed him. He was taken aback a little bit, and pulled away, but then he started kissing me with a violence and fervor that surprised me. His hands were suddenly all over my body, pressing into my groin, clawing at my back. My hard dick throbbed beneath his fingers through the cloth.

I reached for his own crotch, feeling for the size of him. My fingers curved around its shaft and it was as if my hand orgasmed, the muscles themselves so joyed at again feeling cock. With my other hand I started to undo my fly, thinking we were to have sex right there on the couch, but he stopped me. He was a traditionalist, it seemed, and wanted us to move to the bedroom. There was no foreplay for him, he just started undressing himself. I always think there's something really hot to having sex in partial clothing, and to undressing someone slowly, teasingly, but he just stripped right down, even took off his socks. He wasn't finicky about his clothes, like some queens I've had sex with, who need to fold everything neatly or even hang things back in the closet before they climb into bed and turn their attention to having sex. He let his clothes fall where they dropped, and crawled under the covers to wait for me to undress myself.

I watched him as he stripped, playing the voyeur, at least, if I was going to be denied the pleasure of undressing him. It was a very short show, but my neglected dick was aching the entire time. His body was nothing special, pretty much exactly as I'd imagined it, but it was naked and in front of me, and that was something wonderful. His cock was a pleasant surprise, being shorter but thicker than I'd imagined. I thought about going down on it as I stripped out of my own clothing, and my saliva started to flow as I imagined the taste of his cock's flesh, its weighty solidness between my lips.

He lifted the covers for me join him on the bed, and I crawled in beside him. He was all over me, roughly kissing my neck and chest, his stubble rubbing my skin raw, his arms kneading my ass, his cock pressing up against my belly as he wrapped his legs around mine, pinning me to him. I felt half-suffocated, but I yielded to him, and to the sensation of being surrounded by his masculinity. It was unpleasant and yet I wanted every minute of it.

I pushed him away enough to catch my breath and to let me take control of the situation. I wanted his cock, and I rolled him on his back and began licking his nipples. He pushed my head down towards his crotch and I worked my tongue down along the trail of hairs leading to his cock, teasing him. He didn't seem to understand, and kept pushing my head more forcefully towards his cock, lifting it up for my mouth with his other hand. So much for foreplay, I realized, and went down on him right away, taking the head between my lips and lowering myself onto him. I pumped up and down a bit, then pulled off to lick the shaft and his nuts. He grabbed my hair and pulled me back onto his cock, grinding his hips so that he was thrusting into my mouth.

Nothing fancy, then, just the pure hydraulics of sex. Still, I went into almost a trance of cocksucking, so focused on his dick sliding into and out of my mouth. I thought of nothing else--just that meaty organ pumping between my lips, the feel of his cockhead sliding over my tongue, the tickle of his pubic hairs on my lips and chin--and was therefore surprised when I felt his own lips clamp around my cock. He'd swiveled around on the bed so we were locked in a sixty nine, and I slowed my rhythm to match his. (There was no way he'd have noticed enough to match mine.) His mouth was hot and wet, but right then I was so focused on sucking cock, I probably could've come, without even touching myself, just from sucking him.

Suddenly he had a spit-lubed finger up my ass. I hadn't even noticed that he'd stopped sucking me, but I relaxed into his finger and thrust my ass upward a bit more and kept working on his cock. Soon he had a second finger up inside of me, and I was pushing back against his fingers as I worked my lips up and down his cock. He thrust a third finger inside of me, and started saying he wanted to stick his cock in me. I asked for a condom, which he didn't have, so I told him no. He tried to convince me otherwise, but I refused. He was disappointed, and thrust my face back onto his cock, grinding his hips upwards so he was fucking my face.

His finger fucking had brought me close to orgasm, and I licked one palm and began fisting myself as I sucked on his cock. I slipped my tongue between his foreskin and the cockhead, tasting the strong stale scent of him, then took his whole thick cock down my throat as far as my gag reflex would allow, sucking like I could suction the cum out of him. I was dragging my lips up and down his shaft when I came, squirting lines of jism across his legs and the sheets. My lips locked around his thick shaft until I was done, and then my mouth began pumping once again. Soon I felt his balls tighten, ready to explode, and I pulled off and began fisting him. He kept trying to push my head back onto his cock, but I just kept fisting his thick tool in one hand and a moment later he was shooting streams of cum up onto his belly. He didn't have much range, but he made up for it in volume, the white liquid drenching the mat of dark hair that coated his lower torso.

As soon as the sex was over and he'd caught his breath, he jumped out of bed and started putting his clothes on. He didn't clean himself up or anything, just pulled everything on right over the jism, which soaked into his shirt, leaving a large damp spot. He was trying to act as if nothing had happened, although he also kept inviting me back, telling me he had US porn videos if we wanted to watch one. I thanked him but told him I ought to be going. His awkwardness was making the whole affair seem sleazy in some way, but I resisted falling into that line of thought.

He wrote down his phone number and address, and I stuffed it in my backpack when I was out on the street, but I doubted I'd be calling him again. I'd needed him right then, and maybe I'd need him again, but I now knew where to find men.

The city was as hot as ever as I walked across town, but I didn't care. I was riding high on sex and being queer and the taste of cock lingering in my mouth, and that was enough to make me forget all else. My Spanish summer was suddenly looking much more exciting.

I walked to the plaza beneath the Alhambra, and sat down again on a bench in front of the hotel. It was barely one o'clock. There was sure to be another wave of tourists after lunch. Already my cock was beginning to stiffen in my pants as I waited.

And as soon as the siesta was over, I'd buy myself a box of condoms.

YOSHI, HONOLULU, AND THE NEW TATOO
by Michael Lassell

Hawaii is a paradise. Yes, it is–despite the grotesque smear of com-
merce on the gentle lips of Waikiki, where royalty sat under a banyan
tree to welcome the incoming surf; despite the honky-tonk of the tourist
zone, the spoiled innocence of Oahu and the neighbor islands; despite
the constant eruptions of volcanoes and the occasional tidal wave (Hilo
washed away in one morning moment from an earthquake in Alaska);
despite a statehood that bled the island of its intriguing eroticism;
despite generations of naval maneuvers (of all kinds) and the sad
Mainland-izing of a once precious and unique Pacific culture. Still, it's
Edenic. Even in the rain.

I'm standing on the balcony of my five-star hotel, my back to the room,
looking out over across the beach at Diamond Head, waiting.

"Oh, my god!" I gasped out loud when the bellman slid open the louvered doors and I saw the famous land mass for the first time live. I had
seen it before, of course, in photographs, post cards, films (From Here
to Eternity, for example). But there is no preparation for the perfection
of the truncated cone of that extinct volcano, for the size and shape of
it that seems to appease any internal aesthetic discord, that seems to
speak out loud to the spiritual silence inside us all. And it is always
there, this mountain of natural serenity, no matter what non-sense goes
on around it.

    Hawaii is not less a paradise when it is raining. The rain is part of the
paradise of it. Sometimes the drops are large and the showers short,
intense, per haps violent. Sometimes the palm trees bend in gales of

typhoon ferocity, and other times a warm mist seems almost to descend like a particular kind of light from large gray and white clouds that hover on the hillside above the high-rise hotels. The first time I visited Hawaii, it was one of these rains. It lasted for days. It wasn't so much rain as humidity made manifest, but a cooling and refreshing thing, not an enervating one.

It's raining as I wait–for the fifth day in a row. It would be sunset now, if the sun were shining. I haven't seen it since the day I arrived. My room is gorgeous, and I enjoy just being here, sitting on the protected terrace, watching intrepid travel-ers walk in the wet sand. With both sets of sliding doors open on the closet between the bathroom and bedroom, you can see Diamond Head fro the bathtub and shower.

I'm waiting for a masseur to come to my room. When relaxation is my agenda, I relax.

Here's how Honolulu works: First there is Waikiki, a long, shallow crescent of beach on the Mamala Bay, though there's a bump in it as the western end. Beyond the little bump in the crescent is the Ala Wai Yacht Harbor and the Hilton Hawaiian Village hotel complex, near the lagoon where you sometimes can't swim because of the jelly fish, their doings carefully exhibited in the local aquarium, which is down at. the other end, near the Waikiki War Memorial Natatorium, a salt-water pool that's no longer in use, and Queen's Surf Beach (the gay beach), which is near Queen Kapiolani Park. I mean, it's named for an actual monarch, not for the real or imagined effeminacy of the boys in bikinis who are laid out for each other's inspection like moon fish on the piers for the morning chef's auction. In-between are too many hotels and too many tourists, about half of them boiled-lobster Mainland Americans slathered in white creams and coconut-scented oils, and about half of them Japanese in pristine outfits that seem never to have been near water, much less a busy beach.

Among the famous hotels are the Moana, built of wood in 1901, an

Edwardian U around the king's banyan tree (under which Robert Louis Steven-son wrote Kidnapped, despite killer hangovers from the king's all-night card parties at the Iolani Palace). Another is the goofy pink Royal Hawaiian, which is where the cinematic Gidget came to stay with her family back in the '60s. Out-rigger canoes and double-hulled cata-marans carry visitors out into the surf, out where the water is so clear you can see giant turtles swimming alongside and below you.

Behind the beach is King Kalakaua Avenue. It's loud, it's ugly. It's the shill center of the island. All right, Kalakaua Avenue is not paradise.

A block further from the beach is Kuhio Avenue. It's "Old Waikiki," and "the gay district," at least as much as there is one. There are a dozen or so business within a couple of blocks: Hula's Bar & Lei Stand, an indoor-outdoor affair, is the island's most famous rendezvous point for locals, tourists, and military men intent on meeting each other (tell or no tell). At Fusion, a few blocks east down the street, there are strip-pers and female impersonators and a clothing store called 80% Straight somewhere in-between (I bought an earring there that hasn't been out of my lobe since the day I bought it).

There's something about Hawaii I love.

Some elusive thing that includes the notions of soul and immortality and that is not unrelated to sex.

I've been to islands before. None have won me over like this one, even though the others have been as beautiful, less spoiled, less revoltingly American in red, white, blue, and credit cards.

My masseur knocks on the door. I hope it's him. You never know what to expect with a hotel masseur. They can be old-school (tough linea-ment-wielding griz-zled former boxers who learned their craft in down-town gyms) or young and New Age, arriving with aromatic oils, scent-ed candles, redolent herbs, medita-tion music. Some are attractive. Some are gay. I have had sex a surprising number of times with quite legitimate masseurs in some of the finest hotels in the world, the first time with a soft Korean man at the Mandarin Oriental in San Francisco, who said the small mole on the sole of my right foot was a sign of good luck. I guess it was irresistible.

Having sex with a masseur you aren't paying for sex is a compliment. I am flattered by it. At hotels, it's the ultimate amenity.

Today's masseur is the smallest I have ever seen. He's young (in his twenties, I'd guess) maybe five-three. In heels. If he weighs a hundred pounds, I'd be surprised. I'm five-ten and outweigh him two to one–at least. He's so thin, his lips pull off his teeth like an anorexic teenager. I think of photos I have seen of the victims of radiation after the atomic annihilation of Hiroshima and Na gasaki. And I am reminded of my tour of Pearl Harbor earlier in the week, where veterans of the U.S. Navy and veterans of the Imperial Navy of Japan stood side by side on the memorial platform that strides the sunken Missouri and shed tears of identical salt content, and held the hands of their wives, nobody know-ing what to do or who to look in the eye half a century away from the horror that lies under our feet, a rotting metal hulk you can see clearly from the air, a mausoleum where hundreds of bodies were returned to dust through the bellies of Pacific sea creatures.

He tells me his name: Yoshi. It's the John of Japan.

Yoshi is wearing a tight white T-shirt he must have bought in a boys' department somewhere, white stretch pants of the kind gymnasts wear, white socks, white Nikes with a boomerang of robin's-egg blue. The table is as big, and as heavy, as he is. He sets it up flat on the floor, leaving it's legs tucked underneath, in collapsed position (think of a camel's legs when it's down on the sand). This is going to be a shiatsu massage. I've had them before like this, on the floor. It gives the masseur more leverage, more options (including the freedom to walk or crawl up the back of the massagee). I love shiatsu. Unless it's in China, where it's more like revenge than relaxation.

Yoshi has a small boom box with him. He punches a button or two and–yes, soft New Age music begins to clink and ching around the room determined to sound like crystal water drops.

I watch him setting up from the door near the balcony, so as not to be in his way. Yoshi motions me toward the massage table with his head. He doesn't actually speak English. But this hotel is owned by the Japanese, and more of the guests are wealthy tourists from west of Hawaii than from the continent in the east.

I slide the wooden louvered doors closed, leaving the glass sliders open behind them. Privacy... but still open to the soft outdoors and the fall of moisture that is almost rain. Then I drop my robe on the bed and lie down, naked, on my stomach. The relaxing begins in earnest.

When it rains for a long time in Hawaii, which inhabitants say is rare, you can run out of things to do. After all, tourist activities are pitched entirely toward watersports, and you can only spend so much time at the Bishop Museum up in the heights. Even a beautiful room in a luxury hotel can seem confining.

I love my tattoos. First I loved one, then two, but when I looked in the mirror I felt asymmetrical. The small crane medallion on my right shoulder is lower on my arm than the larger chevron of black ribbon on the left. I knew before I came to Hawaii that the solution was a band on my right arm under the small round crane. I wonder if this is the Top arm or the Bottom arm, but I don't care. I'm not into leather or bondage. I'm into visual balance. I was waiting for the where and when. Today was it.

"Where did you get your tattoos?" people frequently ask me, for reasons I am never sure. Where? It's an odd kind of question.

I got the first one in Japan I say (which happens to be a lie; I got it in Los Angeles, on the Sunset Strip near the Mondrian Hotel, but because it's Japanese in style, people believe it); the second one is kind of tribal, so I could get away with saying I got it in Ireland, but I got the second one in L.A., too, so I say so. "The band is from Hawaii," I now get to say of the third one, and it's the truth.

"Some people put decals on their luggage," I like to say, "I get tattoos." It's a testosterone bravado kind of thing to say, I know, particularly since they don't even hurt me. That's something straight sailors made up during World War II to make people at home think they were brave or something, that's all I can think—although everyone says that the closer to the bone you go, the more they hurt. (Tattoos are a lot like love in this.) My tattoos are on my more than amply fleshy arms.

Chinatown in downtown Honolulu, a mile or two from Waikiki, is gentrifying. There are nice little restaurants here now, antiques shops, lei stands. But Hotel Street is still the down-and-out district, especially at night: cheap bars, porn theaters, flesh peddlers—the kind of place that probably should be off-limits to U.S. military, but probably isn't, given the government's rabid pro-heterosexual pose.

Across Smith Street from China Seas Tattoo is a pool hall where the junkies and hookers hang out during the day yelling at each other and smoking each other's cigarettes and pulling on each other's clothes—at least it was there the day I got my third tattoo. If I hadn't seen the work China Seas does, I'd never have gone for it. But there was a picture in the paper this morning of a koi fish of such spectacular beauty on a man's chest and shoulder that I knew as I sat eating breakfast—sparrows nibbling crumbs from my bread in the rain at my feet—that this would be the day. I mentioned it to a woman from the hotel. She knew the man in the paper, a watercress farmer whose small spread was near-by. We jumped into a white hotel van and drove over. Ken was wearing rain gear, big boots because he'd been in the cress beds (like rice, it grows in water). Joyce asked him to show me his tattoo, and he took off his rain coat and long-sleeved thermal undershirt. He was thin, dark, Japanese/Hawaiian, with just a few strands of hair on surprisingly large, dark nipples.

The tattoo was luminescent on his skin, mostly green and black. The de tail of the scales and the shading of it all were breathtaking, at least if you like tattoos, but you already know I do.

The tattoo artist was a disappointment. Old and fat, he hadn't shaven for days, so his face was covered by a coarse white stubble. He was ill-dressed and smoked nonstop, the ash from his unfiltered cigarettes falling on his gut as he worked. My first tattoo was something of a sexual experience, and so was the second. The one that got away (in Limerick) was going to be seriously erotic, but the clock beat us, that last day in Ireland.

"I want a traditional armband," I said.

He grunted.

He took some masking tape, wrapped it around my arm and took a ball-point pen and traced the tape. Then he ripped it off.

"Do you have patterns to look at?" I asked him.

"No," he said. "Every one is different." So he went to work: First he tattooed over the pen lines, then he made two parallel lines inside. Then he started to work on the abstract sharks' teeth and woven-mat designs. Three hours later it was done and I was draped on the netting at the front of a catamaran that was slapping around on the high surf off Waikiki.

"Cool, tat, man," the Hawaiian crewman said in the soft accent of the is lands' patois.

I was thinking about staying in Hawaii. I'd already left the ex in L.A. to move home to New York. Maybe some kind of seriously radical move would be good for me.

"This hurt?" Yoshi asked when he was about to massage my right arm.

"No," I said, "not really. It itches more than hurts."

"Very nice," he said. "I like."

"I like, too," I say and look him straight in the eye.

Here's a thing about being naked and having another man massage my body: Sometimes it turns me on. Usually, it turns me on. Sometimes it turns the masseur on, too. Particularly if the masseur is gay. Here is something else about being naked and aroused under the caring callused hands of a male masseur: Sometimes you have sex, and nobody even has to use the words "gay" or "straight" or even think them or of any other apposition of erroneous opposites.

Here's something else about having a massage: Sometimes the masseur is turning you on on purpose.

Here's how a masseur lets you know he's interested in a little reciprocal friction:

When you are lying on your stomach, he kneels between your legs and massages high... and I mean high ... on the thigh.

When you are lying on your back, he lingers on your nipples in a way no uninterested masseur does.

He leans way over your body from behind your head, rubbing his basket in your face.

He casually brushes a hand against your stiff dick without saying a word.

But someone has to make the first move. He has to touch your well-exposed private parts in an unmistakably motivated way, or you have to touch him–almost anywhere will do. If you are having a massage, and you touch the masseur, and he doesn't move your hand off his arm or leg or crotch, the odds are pretty good that you are about to consummate.

When I am turned on by a massage, it usually starts while I'm still on my stomach. The upper thigh/butt massage part does it. When I flip over, my semi-hard dick, now freed from the weight of my body, just engorges to its full tumescence and bobs up and down on my stomach while the masseur works. Sometimes a masseur uses a sheet or towel to cover the parts he's not working on. Sometimes not. I prefer not, because it leads more often to sex. A sheet is usually a sign that there will be no hanky-panky. Knowing in advance you are not going to have sex with your masseur can be a good thing, too: You relax in a whole different way.

Here's my favorite move.

I am lying there, silently, my dick hard. I'm not objecting to anything the masseur does.

I wait until he's behind me, in this case, kneeling at my head, with one bare thigh on each side of my head–

Oh, did I mention that at some point in this process when my eyes were closed that Yoshi slipped himself out of his Nikes and his athletic socks and his stretch pants and was now wearing only his T-shirt and the thinnest possible white nylon shorts?

The little devil.

I am lying there, silently, my dick hard. I'm not objecting to anything the Yoshi is doing, and he's doing all of everything to drop every hint he can.

He leans over my body and massages down my torso pushing the heels of his hands into my chest and sliding down over the oil past my belly and down to the pubic hair, splitting off at the last possible moment, one hand tracking the inside of each thigh.

Which means his dick is about a quarter of an inch above my face.

I lift my arms up over my head in a stiff-elbowed, Ken-doll kind of pivot from the shoulders. My tattoo feels hot and tight, like a sunburn.

I arch my back and lift my head enough to touch the little bundle of Yoshi that's hovering right in front of me. I push into his crotch with my forehead. He's hard.

That's my cue.

I put one hand on each of his buttcheeks, tiny in my hands and warm un der the cool, white nylon.

Which is his cue to take my dick in his well-oiled hand.

I sigh– a deep sexual sigh.

It's only natural.

I turn my head and take his dick in my mouth through his sorts. His black public hair is poking through the white nylon.

He sighs.

I notice that there is no difference between a middle-aged Anglo-American sigh and a much younger Japanese one.

I reach behind his back and pull his shirt up over his head.

Then I lift him, in an easy single gesture, around to the front of me. There is a momentary awkwardness involving legs and getting the shorts off him, but it's done with enough finesse not to break our concentration, and now he is naked, too.

His dick—uncut, of course—is so thin I think at first it's small. But it's longer, and now longer, and now longer, and it feels very good in my mouth. His balls are small. The head of his dick is incredibly smooth in my mouth; his nipples are hardening between my fingers.

The king-sized bed is only a foot away. It seems like a waste not to take advantage of it. So we do.

Suddenly the sex becomes passionate and specific (or maybe it's the other way around as cause and effect). It is now no longer an anonymous fantasy masseur, but this small, thin Yoshi who is turning me on, and I can't get enough of him into my mouth. I can't get my tongue far enough into his asshole (the way he's groaning I'm guessing he's fairly new to being rimmed by an enthusiastic bearded man).

We shift again so he can get me into his mouth, which is, sad to say, too small to take me very far in, but I'm not complaining, really.

We wind up with him on top, sitting on my dick, which is rubbing like an independent force against his ass crack. In another decade I'd have that thing spit-slick and up his asshole to the red pubic hair before he could object (or thank me), but this is the '90s. Still, there's no way stopping to find a condom, which could freak him out and queer the whole thing, so to speak, or at the very least turn me soft as a well-massaged gluteus max, and I'm not willing to risk it.

He's making little noises which might be Japanese or might not be language at all, at least not in the usual sense, although I'm getting that he's getting ready to shoot, which is fine with me. Its why I'm jerking him off as fast and hard as I can.

And that's how we come. He starts to shoot and starts to put his hand over his dick and I pull it away and let him spurt into the long untrimmed bush of hair on my chest, and when he's done, I pull him off me, settle him into the nest between the crook of my left arm and my body, and finish myself off with my right hand in a geyser that shocks him, satisfies me, and drenches us both.

It's not until we're both lying there breathing a little less heavy, and soaking wet in our East-meets-West cum that I kiss him for the first time, and he kisses back, gently–gentler than the music or the scent of ginger blossoms in the afternoon rain.

We kiss some more in the giant glass box of a shower, about the size of a walk-in closet.

"I not supposed to do," he says at some point while I am soaping up his back and between his thighs, either asking me in his way not to blow the whistle or assuring me that this is not part of his usual reper-toire of relaxation moves (although it was not all that dissimilar to other shiatsu massages I've had, the first on the floor of the living room in a suite at the Biltmore on Pershing Square in Los Angeles).

"Well, don't worry," I tell him, "I'm not going to tell."

But then, I guess I do, at the remove of several years now, and enough anonymity (I hope) that he won't get into trouble, if he hasn't already.

So maybe Yoshi is why I like Hawaii, or maybe it's the actual sex masseur from the night before (who was way less expert at sex or mas-sage than Yoshi), or maybe it was the Saturday-night strippers at Fusion, who like you to look at their dicks when you drop a dollar into their g-strings and to take a liberal squeeze of anything you choose. Or maybe it was the very not gay crewman on that sail boat on the Windward side who told me he got his earring at 80% Straight and never even batted a self-conscious eyebrow ,or the Day-glo rainbow of reef fish at Haunama Bay (you can see it in Blue Hawaii), though one of them actually bit me on the dick when I took it out of my Speedos to pee–no, seriously, deep enough to make the glans bleed and hard enough to leave a mouth-shaped bruise the next day that hurt more than the healing tattoo in salt water. Or may-be it's the tattoo itself that makes me love Hawaii, a tattoo that every day re-minds me not just of Waikiki and Kuhio Street and the Seven Seas tattoo parlor, but of Yoshi, the minuscule Japanese masseur, and a very good time we had on the sixteenth floor of a view hotel on Oahu, a mile or two from Diamond Head on a misty January afternoon.

REMEMBERING
by Tom Caffrey

When I was a child, I had a recurring dream in which a man was staying at our house for the night. I didn't know his name or why he was there. I didn't know anything about him except that for some reason he excited me in a way no one else ever had. Hearing his voice would make me tremble, and when he touched my arm to say goodnight, the warmth he left behind was deeper than that of any fire.

In this dream, I fell asleep feeling the man's presence in the house, as though despite the walls that separated us he was holding me in his arms. In the morning, he would be gone, leaving behind a well-worn T-shirt on his bed. I would pull the shirt over my head and be immediately surrounded by the smell and heat of him. It was intoxicating. My head would swim as I breathed in his scent and felt the shirt, which had fit so tightly on his large body, float around my smaller one. Inevitably, I would wake from the dream to sticky sheets and a breathlessness born of unnamed desire.

No man ever left me his shirt in those days, but many have since. I have a drawer filled with them, a drawer I never open. I like to know that it's there, that inside are collected, like the discarded skins of wild animals, the shirts of men whose bodies I have felt sliding against mine as their cocks entered my ass, men whose mouths have closed over mine as they spilled their loads deep inside me, and whose fingers have gripped my wrists above my head as they led me once again into those adolescent dreams.

The shirts are stained--with sweat and come and sometimes the faint scent of soap--and each holds the smell of its owner tightly in its arms. I do not take them out, because there is memory in objects, and I do not want the memories to fade. I prefer to keep them, neatly folded, in their drawer. Sometimes as I pass the dresser I feel their presence, and sometimes on summer nights I can smell their fragrance rising from the drawer like the breath of the flowers comes from the garden below my window. On those night I wake, as I did when I was twelve, with my cock hard in my hand and my mind swimming with the memories of men.

There is one thing I do allow myself to touch. It is a jacket, made of black leather and much like any mother motorcycle jacket seen on any number of men. But it is also unlike all other jackets, in that it belonged to one man not like any other man I have ever known. A man I wanted more than I have ever wanted anything.

The jacket hangs in my bedroom closet, towards the back, hidden behind rows of neatly-pressed dress shirts. I do not look at it often, fearing that overuse will cause the memories to fade. I cannot risk forgetting. Knowing it is there is usually enough. But sometimes, especially when the air begins to change from the warm breezes of summer to the crisp breath of fall, just knowing is no longer enough. That's when I reach inside and, feeling the smooth leather beneath my fingers, it all comes back...

I saw Jesse for the first time on an October night. I had been working late at the bookstore, and it was after midnight when I finally finished and locked up. It was one of the first cold nights of the season, and I remember very clearly the way the way the wind felt as it played around my face. The moon overhead was almost full, and as I walked towards home, everything seemed to be glazed with a covering of soft, bewitching gold.

Dunstable is a small college town, the kind found scattered all throughout New England like rice at a wedding. It began life as a small fishing port, which over the years changed personas several times as fishing died and the people were forced to find different ways of life. Unlike other towns in the northeast, it did not have the advantage of being either the scene of a witchcraft panic or the site of an historic uprising, so it had to make do with what it had, which was it's quiet and its beauty. When Farley University set up house and the people began to come, first with their big ideas and later with their Volvos and their PhDs, the town found its true calling, and embraced this new way of life as it had all the others before it.

Since then, the town had grown to surround the University. A new world of coffee houses, meditation centers, and bookstores was built alongside the fish markets and auto shops, and within a decade no one would ever remember that once it had been different. The town had settled into a cycle of seasons that easily became familiar to anyone who stayed there for more than a year. I noticed Jesse precisely because he did not fit into Dunstable's normal pattern of life. He appeared in my vision as something out of place, perhaps even out of time, breaking the ordinariness of my nightly walk home. Where usually I would see nothing but the smooth brick face of the wall next to the Black Sheep Pub, I saw instead a man leaning against the stone in a waterfall of electric light, watching me.

It surprises me now that I sensed no fear. If anyone told me a story that began with their chancing upon a stranger after midnight, I would immediately suspect some sinister motive behind it all. But it wasn't like that. Maybe it was the spell of the first autumn night, or perhaps just that after almost a decade in Dunstable I was incapable of thinking in terms of imminent danger. Whatever the cause, I simply nodded and said "Hello."

Jesse, although of course I didn't yet know his name, responded with a nod of his own, but he remained silent, watching me as I walked past him. While I didn't stare at him, I did glance long enough to take in his appearance. Tall and broad, he was wearing jeans and black boots. His upper body was wrapped in a leather jacket. He looked, in fact, like a lot of the boys who attended Farley, many of whom tried to adopt an aura of what I guessed they assumed was hypermasculine sexiness simply by putting on a motorcycle jacket plucked off the rack at James

Dean's Closet.

Sometimes I would go to these young men, waiting in bathroom stalls or under the trees in the park, and suck their dicks. As I moved over the lengths of their cocks, I let my hands play over their jackets, only to find the surfaces stiff with newness, the zippers stubborn with disuse. Then I would bring them off quickly, with no desire or pretense of need, and leave before they'd even finished coming. Their posing disgusted me, their attempts at taking on what they would never earn leaving me cold.

Only Jesse was no pretender. He looked like he'd been born in his boots and jacket. I could tell by the way he stood that he wore them with the confidence of someone whose body demanded them, that every crease and fold had been put there by experience. And I knew instinctively that he wouldn't look quite right in anything else. On his body, anything besides jeans and that jacket would always appear the wrong size, no matter how carefully it was tailored. It was he who made the leather come alive, and not the other way around. That, and not his strangeness, is what made him dangerous to me.

I hurried past him and made my way down the street. I knew he was watching me, and that he knew I was thinking about him. It was as though there was nothing else I could be doing, even if I wanted to. I tried to think of anything else--the night's receipts, the author arriving for a signing the next day, the leftover roast beef in the refrigerator. But his presence filled up all of the empty air around me until, halfway down the block, I was forced to turn around.

He was waiting for me. Still leaning against the wall, he had hunted me down with his eyes as I'd tried to escape. Now, even in the dark, I knew they were focused on me. I moved slowly, as if in water, retracing my path until I was only a few feet from where he stood. As I approached, he smiled. "Come on," he said, and I followed.

He led me to the alley that ran between the Black Sheep and my store. Stepping into it, he was swallowed by the darkness, and for a moment I thought about just running away, back to the safety of my well-lit home and the security of a rooms filled with familiar things. But then I remembered the way his jacket moved around him, and I slipped into the night behind him.

The alley was narrow, flanked on either side by the high brick walls of the buildings. The moon overhead shone down between them, creating a thin river of golden light that ran between the brick banks. It was in this river that Jesse and I moved. He turned to me and pressed me against the wall. I felt the coldness of the bricks against my hands and the weight of his body against my chest.

"Tell me what you want," he said.

I looked into his dark eyes. His face, I saw now, was almost boyish, with pale skin and full lips. But he was no boy. The strength in the hands that pinned me was that of a man, a man who knew what he was doing.

"I want to taste you," I said at last.

Jesse smiled. "That's what I thought," he said, and kissed me. His tongue slammed against mine, pushing its way inside. His hands were in my hair, pulling my head back as he ground against my body. I felt his knee move between my legs and press up into my groin.

My hands freed, I reached out and touched the skin of his jacket. The leather was cool with night, and as soft as Jesse's kisses were rough. My hands moved over his arms and back slowly, searching out every curve of the body beneath the second skin. They traced the edge of his collar, treading the line between flesh and leather, between the warmth of blood and the smoothness of the jacket.

I moved my mouth away from Jesse's and down his throat, my tongue running over unshaven skin until it reached the top of his jacket. When I tasted the rich sensation of leather, I put my hands on his waist and began to lick the edges of the zipper holding the jacket closed. The metal scraped lightly on my teeth as I moved down, sinking until I was on my knees, looking up at Jesse. My hands rested on his boots.

"Please," I said.

Jesse looked down at me, then reached for his zipper. He pulled it down, opening his jacket. Underneath he wore just a plain white T-shirt. I reached up and undid the buckle of his wide leather belt, then pulled at the buttons holding his jeans closed. They slid open easily, sliding down his muscular legs to his knees. He was wearing a jockstrap. The thin bands crossed the mounds of his ass, stretched tightly. The pouch hung down, weighted with his cock and balls.

Leaning forward, I ran my hands up under his T-shirt, feeling a thick cover of hair on his belly. My mouth worked on his pouch, sucking at the hidden prick. I could smell him in the material, and breathed deeply. It was the smell of a man, heavy and rich, and it filled my nose as I licked hungrily at his balls.

Moving my hands around to Jesse's back, I slid the jockstrap down, feeling his ass fill my hands. Tugging it down in front, I freed his cock, which sprang up half hard over a pair of juicy balls. I took it into my mouth, slipping the tip inside my lips and sucking softly. I could feel the blood beating in his shaft as his dick filled with heat and swelled to its full length.

Jesse pushed against me, sliding deep into my throat. The heat of his skin surrounded me as I took him in, so different from the coolness of the air around us. My lips moved over his shaft, sucking at his hard flesh while his swollen head filled my throat. His hands gripped my shoulders steadily as he pumped himself in and out of my mouth.

I sucked Jesse for what seemed like an eternity, savoring the taste of his skin, the smell of him when I buried my nose in his thick bush. From time to time I ran my hands over his boots, sucking harder when I had the leather under my hands, as though drawing my need from it.

Then Jesse pulled out. "Stand up," he said, and I obeyed. "Now strip."

Oblivious to the cold, I pulled my clothes off, dropping them to the ground. In a minute I was standing naked in front of Jesse, the wind raising a chill up and down my exposed skin as I waited.

Jesse stepped forward and grabbed my cock in his hand. He

squeezed hard, making me gasp. Until that moment, I hadn't even realized how hard I was. Jesse's fingers on my prick almost made me
shoot. Even more beautiful was the feeling of his jacket against my
naked skin.

"Turn around."

I turned, and Jesse pushed me forward so that I was leaning against
the wall. He moved in behind me, putting his arms around my chest. I
could feel his cock pressed against my ass. I bent my head forward and
felt leather beneath my cheek. Jesse began to thrust, rubbing his dick
up and down the crack of my ass. The small metal teeth of his zipper
scraped against my sides as he moved, drawing forth tiny fingers of
pleasure.

I ran my tongue over the sleeve of his jacket. His hands held me
tightly, and the touch of leather pressed against my naked skin made
me want him more than I'd ever wanted anything. The fact that he was
teasing me with his cock was almost too much.

"Please," I whispered. "Please fuck me."

But he didn't. He just pushed against me ever harder, until I was
almost shaking from his touch. I was sucking at the sleeve of his jacket, licking the surface, biting at the small snaps at the cuffs. Behind me,
the head of his dick taunted me with every push.

Then he was inside me. Pulling back, he found the opening of my
hole and drove home. My head flew back as he entered, and I felt his
arm around my throat, blocking my cries. I bit the sleeve of his jacket
where it pressed against my mouth.

Then he began to fuck me, in long, slow strokes. As his rhythm filled
my body, I began to shake. The pressure of his cock as it slid in and
out of my ass brought everything into sharper focus. I felt the coldness
of the air and the softness of his jacket. I drew the night air into my
lungs and smelled mixed within it the scent of leather and desire.

I pushed back against Jesse, asking him to ride me harder. He
answered by building to a fierce rhythm, slapping against my ass
roughly. His arms remained around my chest, pulling me back against

his thrusts and driving him deep inside me. When he came, he tightened his grip on my chest, pushing up into me in short jabs as his load spurted into me.

When he was done, he pulled out and turned me around. "Come on me," he ordered. He stood close to me, his hand on my shoulder, his booted foot pressed against my leg.

For the first time, I touched my own cock. Looking into Jesse's face, and feeling the leather against me, it didn't take me long to bring myself off. With a few tugs on my dick, I watched as a heavy load splattered over the surface of Jesse's jacket and dripped onto his boots. The cum lay pale and white against the darkness of the leather. Jesse ran his finger through the stains, rubbing my cum into the leather. He was smiling.

I saw Jesse many other nights after that one, until I knew the feeling of his body against mine as well as I did that of a familiar shirt. Even now the smell of him lingers in the jacket, left on my bed the morning he had to leave for good. I take it from the closet and pull it over my bare skin. My cock stiffens, and as my hand begins to slide up and down my shaft, I remember everything.

FOR THE RECORD
by Jameson Currier

Dear Editor:

I am twenty-four years old, five feet, ten inches and have a nine inch dick that is 5-3/4 inches around. I am including the size of my dick because I am a faithful reader of your magazine and I can't help but notice that a lot of your stories focus on large dicks and that the writers give these characters dick measurements such as nine, ten, eleven and twelve inches. I would like to know how the writers of these stories are measuring their characters' dicks. Where do they consider the beginning of their measurement -- at the base of the cock? From the top or the bottom of the shaft? I know in a lot of the photo spreads, whenever it reads in a caption something like, "Cliff is nine inches of fun," that he's more like nine inches of imagination because of the way the camera angle distorts the size of his dick in the photograph. Where do these guys begin their measurement? Or are the writers measuring the models' dicks too?

I've known some large dicks in my time, and not just my own, and I'd like it known for the record that a hard dick should be measured along the top of the shaft, with the end of the tape measure placed against the guy's groin. It should not be measured along the underside of the balls, around the balls, wrapping the tape measure around the tip of his dick after starting on the underside, include the circumference of the dick, or, in some porn star cases, with the tape measure shoved six inches up the guy's ass before even getting it up and around to his balls and dick. Quite simply, the size of a dick is from the belly to the tip on the top.

Now, I'd also like it known for the record that because I've got a big dick I can suck myself off and I happen to enjoy doing it. I've never told this to anyone except one other person and that was another guy who could also suck himself off. The night I met him I sucked myself off for him and then he did himself for me. It was fantastic. Unfortunately, we never saw each other again. Well, at least you can say it was safe sex (or safe suck, yuck, yuck).

Now sucking yourself off and enjoying it has become about as misinterpreted as measuring your dick has, but I'd like it known for the record that it is almost as exciting as giving head to another guy. I don't understand why most guys can't do this, unless they're too old or too fat, though the other guy I met who could also do it said that the spinal cord is just not that flexible for some people. Pity, they don't know what they're missing. I'm sure that if most guys could do this little party trick, they'd spend most of their lives with their heads buried in their own crotches instead of trying to brag about the size of it to someone else.

Sincerely,

   The Real Thing

*   *   *

Dear Editor:

I wrote you some time ago about how to measure a dick correctly and since that time I've had to straighten out a lot of guys myself (and which I might also add I thoroughly enjoyed it since I bent most of them out of shape because they didn't measure up to their expectations of themselves). In case you forgot, the correct way to measure a hard dick is from on the top side of the shaft from the groin to the tip of the head. My last boyfriend was particularly upset with me when the eight inches he professed to be was less than seven when it was measured with the right method. It got him so aggravated that he set out trying to find ways of making himself bigger.

He tried a variety of things to make himself longer and for the record let me tell you that none of those pumps or lotions or herbal teas or leather straps with weights really do any good (I know because he tried them all -- and the weights were pretty painful when they were worn because I tried them out, too, just to see what he was complaining about), and the idea of surgical implants and enlargements were really too frightening for him to consider, and I certainly wouldn't want to consider that course myself -- even if I had to. But I would like to tell you and your readers that there are several ways in which you can make yourself look bigger than you really are, and you don't have to hire some fancy-shmancy porno photographer to get you to contort your body into a weird angle to do the trick.

First of all, the closer you trim your pubic hair to the skin the larger the shaft of your dick is going to look. I personally recommend that you don't shave your groin right down to the skin, because it really looks too unnatural and the stubble growing back can be particularly painful for you and your partner. God put a bush there for one reason or another and there's no reason not to keep the garden from growing, you know what I mean? I do recommend, however, that you consider shaving your balls. The cleaner, smoother look down there just helps the dick look like it's hanging lower instead of some straggly, stray pubic hair hanging down there showing it up. A tight, flat stomach is also a bonus for making a dick look longer -- those unflattering rolls of fat just sit there on top of your dick taking up all that space. And finally, a good, clean tan line, bikini or otherwise, for those who can get one, really helps direct the eye to the focal point of a dick -- big, thick, long or otherwise - and will, nonetheless, do a lot for the esteem of those who need it.

After my boyfriend got over the shock of his loss of length and his impractical toy-and-homeopathic driven methods had failed him, he tried my advice, and lo and behold, he did look bigger to me (but no matter how he measured it, according to my rules, he never made it back to being eight inches). I tried to tell him that there are other things to a guy besides just a big dick and I did everything I could to pump up his ego -- he had a much better body than I did, arms like Jean Claude Van Dam, and a beautiful face -- gray eyes and long, floppy black hair. He was a really hot guy and the sex was great between us, though I usually ended up being the bottom more often than not because he was a little intimidated by my size. It fell apart for us, however, the night that I showed him my I-can suck-my-own-dick trick. He was out of the house before I could pull my dick out of my mouth, screaming at the top of his lungs 'what do you need me for if you can do that yourself?'

I'd like it known for the record that every boyfriend I've ever had -- and I've had a few -- has lasted longer the longer he's been, which leads me to believe that it's easier to like a guy with a dick the same size as your-self.

Sincerely,

   The Real Thing

*   *   *

Dear Editor:

I wrote you a few months ago after having lost a boyfriend because of my "size element" and I'm writing to let you know that I've finally met a guy that my larger-than-his-is endowment does not cause any jealousy. He's two years younger than me and his dick is two inches smaller, but he is a really wild thing in bed, so much so that there are days when I walk around with my big dick just aching from so much action. And I haven't been allowed to pull my I-can-suck-my-own dick trick for him after the first time I showed it to him. He said that if I put that thing in my mouth one more time, he'd be out-a-here faster than he can jerk himself off, because every time I pulled that stunt I was depriving him of the pleasure of sucking on my dick.

My new boyfriend can also shoot farther than anyone else he's ever been with and anyone else that I know of, for that matter; he's certainly got me beat in that department. I don't know what the record is for the longest recorded cum shot, but he would certainly vie for top honors. So far he's hit his earlobe, his chin, my forehead and the lamp on my nighttable. And not just the first spurt either -- the guy just cums and shoots and cums and shoots. It's like a fucking water pistol!

For the record, I'd like to share with you and your readers a position we tumbled into last week -- he was able to fuck me at the same time I was fucking him.

This was how it was done. He was in an open scissors-like position fucking me. I opened my legs up, also into an open scissors position. I brought my legs down against the mattress of the bed, wrapped my dick beneath his balls and up into his ass. It wasn't exactly the most comfortable position for me, and we had to have plenty of lube right there on the bed with us, but when I did it, when I got myself inside him while he was inside me, his body just about exploded. I wouldn't recommend this to anyone to try on a first date, but I should probably let you know, when my boyfriend reached an orgasm that night, he shot his cum so far that it hit the ceiling and he said he loved me.

Blissfully,

The Real Thing

KISSING COUSINS
by Walter Wilde

I.

We're sitting out on the back porch, watching the girls play after dinner. It's finally warm enough to really enjoy the evening.

My wife says, "Oh, your cousin, Bobby, called today. He said he and Billy were going camping up at Millstone a week from Saturday. He says they'd like you to come."

I feel my asshole start to tingle. So it's that time of year again.

Billy and Bobby and me have been going camping together three or four times every summer for the last twenty-five years. And for more than fifteen of those years, they've been fucking me up the ass. They've got the only two dicks in the world that've ever been up there, and we've never done any other kind of messing around--cocksucking or anything like that. Far as I know, during the rest of the year, they don't screw any other guy's butts, and I can tell you, I don't go cruising around looking for cocks to bang my hole. I'm just not interested. But with Billy and Bobby, I don't know, it's just kind of a tradition, something we've shared for years. We go out there in the woods and do some fishing and drink a little Wild Turkey and tell dirty jokes and horse around and one thing just leads to another and half-a-dozen times over the three or four days, their boners pop out and my pants come down and I stick my fanny in the air and they ream it out. Sometimes just one of them fucks me, but usually, it's both of them. Especially if it's Billy who's porking me, Bobby gets so turned on watching his big brother ram his cock up my hole that he has to get his piece of ass too right then and there.

They've got very different dicks. Bobby's sticks straight out of his bush and it's almost the shape of a cone--narrow at the top but real thick at the base. Billy's is different. It's maybe not as big as Bobby's at its thickest, but it's longer, and it's got this incredible head on it. His dickhead must be size of a ripe plum. The other thing about it is the curve. It's sort of bowed-like, like one of those Arab swords.

We never talk about how they fuck me, and they never razz me about how I'm the one who gets screwed. It's just something we do every summer. They like it, and I like it--that heft of a solid piece of manmeat deep in my gut. We're as close as brothers, and I guess we just look on it as one of things that makes us closer.

II.

A week from Saturday, Bobby swings by in his pickup and I throw my stuff in the back and hop in. It's been since Christmas since we've seen each other. He lives downstate, selling cars. He's starting to get a little paunchy--too much beer--though hell, all three of us are past thirty-five now. Still, I've kept up my swimming at the city plunge every day--I went to the state championships in high school--and about six months ago started working with weights. Bobby wasn't much into sports like Billy and me. But shit, even with a few extra pounds, Bobby's the same as always--stocky and smiley and ready to please.

Anyhow, I catch him up on Marge and my girls, and he catches me up on Alice and his girls. The only one of us who ever had a boy was Billy--and that was just his first one, Billy Junior. All of his and Lois's after that were girls, too. Bobby gets to bitching about politics and I just kind of nod and watch the countryside roll by. It's about two hours to Millstone, so there's plenty of time for him to get all his notions of how this country ought to be run off his chest.

Bobby was actually the first one to fuck me. It turned out Billy'd been trying to screw him off and on for a couple years, but Bobby didn't like it one bit, so the two of them cooked up a plan to see if maybe one of them could get up my asshole on our next camping trip. Like I said, we'd been going out in the woods together by then for years. Of course, I didn't know what they had in mind. I was still nineteen, Billy was twenty-two, Bobby had just turned eighteen. One afternoon, we were kind of rough-housing around. Billy got me down with my face in the dirt and was sitting on my shoulders. All three of us were laughing like crazy. We were always wrestling around and that kind of stuff.

Anyway, Billy's got me pinned, and he says to Bobby. "Hey, Bobby! Pull down his pants!"

I felt Bobby's fingers undoing my shorts, and I started to struggle some more. It wasn't that I didn't want them to see me bareass. Hell, we'd just been skinnydipping a couple hours before. But that kind of horsing around always gave me half-a-hardon, and I didn't want them noticing that and maybe kidding me about being turned on or something.

"Hey, come on. What're you doing!"

I thought probably they were just going to spank me. We'd do that sometimes too, when we were messing around. Two of us would gang up on the third one and pants him and then smack his buns a little. Just games, you know, nothing serious. Bobby and I'd done it to Billy the first day out. I'd laid a couple solid whacks on that hairy ass of his, and figured maybe this was just getting even.

I was squirming around a lot, and kicking my legs, but Bobby'd managed to get my pants off. Billy had his butt planted on my neck and shoulders, so I really couldn't get up. I was waiting for that first whack on my buns when, all of a sudden, Billy did something he'd never done before. He snaked his hand down and grabbed hold of my balls.

"Cut your wiggling, Tommy," he gave my balls a squeeze, "Cut it out!"

"OW!"

He really yanked my nards.

"That's better. Now stick your butt up. Bobby wants to see your asshole, don't you, Bobby?"

"Yeah."

I wasn't into this, but Billy had me by the balls. I raised up on my knees and pulled my thighs apart so my ass spread wide open. If he wanted a look at my pucker, he was sure going to get a panoramic view.

Billy let out a laugh. "Well, Bobby," he said, "What do you think?"

All Bobby said was, "Wow!"

"So get with it. I ain't gonna sit here and hold Tommy's balls all day!"

I couldn't see what was happening with my face pushed down in the dirt and Billy's butt planted on my neck. But then, I felt something, something hard, pushing against my asshole.

Shit! Bobby was trying to fuck me.

"What the hell!" I started to buck like crazy, trying to throw Billy off, but he just sat down harder, and he started twisting my balls till I thought he'd rip them out by the roots.

I've got real low hangers, and they're real sensitive.

"Just hold still, Tommy. Hold still!"

"OOWW!"

He squeezed so hard I saw stars.

"Okay, good," he said, "Come on, Bobby. Use some spit, you stupid dick."

I heard Bobby spit in his hand, and then felt his gooey fingers right around my butthole, then up inside it.

"Noooo! Billy! Bobby, Noooo!"

"Go ahead," Billy said.

The hot head of Bobby's eighteen year old dick was right there at the mouth of my nineteen year old hole, and then he started to push it up inside me.

"Oww! OWWW! Cut it out!"

But Bobby just kept at it. He jiggered his dick every which way, forcing it up my virgin pucker. I tried to struggle, but Billy'd just give my nards a yank if I started getting too wild. About all I could do was moan and groan while Billy worked his cock up my ass. It seemed like it took five minutes before he got it all jammed in. I could feel him way down deep in my gut, and my buttlips screaming around that thick dickbase he's got.

There was this long pause then.

"So, fuck him, asshole," Billy said, exasperated.

Bobby start to pushed his stick in and out, pretty slow at first. It really burned. My butthole felt like it was being swabbed out with acid or something. I thrashed around, out of breath, "Owww! Cut it out! Nooo! OWWW!"

But Bobby keep porking, getting more and more into it, really pumping my hole. Then, something happened. Billy let go of my balls and grabbed my dick and started to stroke it. I got a boner in about four seconds. When he could feel that, then his fingers just went crazy. He pumped my teenage dick like it was his own.

And suddenly, I wasn't complaining anymore. My asshole didn't exactly burn now. It felt stretched and open and hot, and Bobby's dick, every time he shoved it in to the hilt, hit some spot in my insides that just made my own cock get harder and harder. I was getting some kind of pleasure I never knew before.

"Ohh! Ohh! What're you guys doing to me. Ohhh! Ohhh!"

Billy worked my cock even harder, and Bobby started to ram my butthole like there was no tomorrow.

"Ahhh! Ohhh! Ahhh! I'm shooting. AHHH!" Bobby let out a shout and his dick battered me like crazy, "AHHH!"

I felt something warm and heavy spreading up my insides.

"Get your cock out and get over here," Billy snapped as soon as Bobby's cries had died down, "Jerk his dick." I felt Bobby's cock pop out of my hole, and Billy's weight lifted off my shoulders. I was so dazed and so turned on I didn't even try to get up. There was a new hand around my throbbing pole, and then I felt the head of Billy's dick against my buttlips. Even with his brother's reaming me open, it took him a minute to get that head up me. But then he slid in clean as a whistle.

Bobby brought me off two times with his hand while his brother fucked me.

It was a little tough afterwards, of course. I was ashamed and freaked out and they were both a little shocked at what they'd done. I was going to take off at first, and I called them every name I could think of and told them if I ever laid eyes on either of them again I'd kill them. They were both real apologetic and said they were just funning around and it didn't mean anything.

"Hell," Billy said, "I mean, we're cousins. It's just between us, you know." He looked at me, "I mean, we all got off. You kinda liked it, too. Hell, it's just a new way of playing for us."

That night, they both fucked me again. And that time, they didn't have to hold me down.

III.

We pulled into the parking lot at Millstone about eleven-thirty. As we turned off the highway, all of sudden my dick was hard, and every few seconds, my asshole would kind of spasm. It had been like that ever since that first time my cousins fucked me. It was like my body knew it was almost time for those special mangames we played.

Billy's Chevy was there. There weren't too many cars, since it was still early in the season. Bobby and I got out and looked around to see if we could find him.

"Uncle Bobby! Uncle Tommy!"

What the...

We turned around, and there was Billy Junior. "Well, shit!" Bobby said under his breath. Even though we never said a word about it, you could figure Bobby's been thinking we were going to have some of that fun we only got on camping trips. "What the hell's he doing here."

Billy Junior walked over to us. He wasn't a big kid anymore. He'd just finished his first year of college, where according to his father, he was doing real well. He didn't look much like Billy, who was tall and brown haired. Billy Junior took after his mother's people. He was stocky and red headed, with smooth, fair skin and green eyes.

"Howdy," he said when he got up to us. "Dad's over helping some guy change a tire. He'll be back in just a second."

We stood there kind of uncomfortable for a minute. This looked like it was going to sort of change our traditions. "Gee, Billy Junior"--which is what we always called him--"didn't know you were coming up for the trip, too," Bobby said.

He shrugged. "Well, I had to talk Dad into it. But finally he said it would be okay. I just figured it would be fun to be out with you guys" he smiled, "you know, grown up stuff and all."

There was something kind of dear about the kid, I had to admit, and his Dad couldn't have very well told him the reason he wasn't welcome. Well, maybe Bobby and I could sneak in a little cornholing anyhow off in the bushes.

"Hey!"

Billy came over from the far side of the parking lot. He was looking fit as ever. Unlike Bobby, he really worked at keeping himself up; belonged to some fancy gym where they did aerobics and had machines and all that kind of shit. He'd grown as moustache since I last saw him.

"Hey, come on," he said, "Let's get our butts moving. If we get with it, we can find our spot and set up before sunset."

Bobby looked at me and shrugged. We got the equipment and headed into the woods.

Hiking in, we exchanged news. At one point, Bobby and Billy dropped behind, and when I looked back, I could see Bobby throwing his arms around angrily, probably bitching at Billy for bringing Billy Junior along. I was walking with the boy and asked him how school was going, and he told me about his classes and the girl he was dating and playing rugby, which he'd never done before and really liked. He said it was a real rough game with lots of action and body contact--"a game for real studs," he called it--and he was proud of being the youngest member of the team. He was in that kind of good shape that's natural in a kid that age, broad shoulders and a tight little fanny, his muscles taut and firm, but with a hint of that baby-fat still to him.

"You know, Uncle Tommy," (he always called me "uncle," since it really was just like I was Billy and Bobby's brother) "I didn't think Dad was going to let me come. He said you guys had been doing this so long that he didn't know how you'd feel about it. You and Uncle Bobby aren't pissed, are you? I just kind of wanted to be around you guys, you know." He looked at me real seriously, "I mean, I didn't say this to Dad, but I guess I kind of wanted to feel like now I was kind of one of the men in the family, too."

Hell, what was I going to say. I looked into that anxious face that still was pretty much a boy's. I guess there's that fancy word, "ingenuous," that describes it pretty well.

"Shit, Billy Junior, we're not mad. It just that your Dad didn't say anything about you coming. But it's great to have you along."

I glanced back again. Bobby was listening to Billy. I guess he'd gotten his anger out. I shook my head. Pretty soon he'd probably start up on politics.

By the time we found a good site, got the camp set up, a fire going and some dinner cooked, we were pretty bushed. Usually, the first night, we didn't mess around anyway. I wondered if maybe, next day, Bobby and I might sneak off and get it on a little. Even after what I'd said to Billy Junior, there was still no question that I was disappointed. Like I said, I don't get fucked by other guys. But I'd been getting ploughed by my cousins every summer for years, and I don't mind admitting my asshole really had been looking forward to it.

Next morning, we got up with the birds. All four of us had boners, including the boy, and we kind of razzed each other about them as we wandered off in the bushes for our morning piss. Bobby and me were taking our leaks side by side and Bobby winked at me and said that in the mornings he was always so horny nobody should get within ten feet of him. From back behind us, I could hear Billy Junior say over the patter of our piss, "Yeah, me too, Uncle Bobby. It must run in the family."

I shook my head. If that boy had any notion of what Bobby had in mind...

By seven-thirty or so, we were dressed and had had breakfast and were all set for the day.

"I'm going to take Billy Junior with me," Bobby said, "We're going to hike over that rise there to that creek about three miles up, remember? I always had good fishing up there."

"Fine with me," Billy said, "Tommy and me'll just hang out for a while and get some wood together for the fire tonight, and then maybe we'll join you."

"Okay."

Bobby and the boy headed out. Billy and I policed the site, and then I heard him say, kind of soft, "Hey, Tommy..."

I looked up. He was waving me over to the middle of the camp, "Get your ass over here. I want to mess around a little."

I didn't have to be asked twice. If we were going to play around at all, it was going to have to be on the sly like this. Billy already had that amazing dick of his out of his pants. Lord, that head of it was impressive, and that curve really did make it look like a weapon. I hustled over and pulled down my pants. My own hardon flopped out stiff as a sausage.

"You don't think they'll be back or anything?" I said.

"No," he said, "I told Bobby to make sure they were gone at least till noon. Then I'll take the boy off and the two of you can have some fun." He turned me around and pushed me down on all fours and knelt down behind me. He ran his hand all over my hairy cheeks. "Jeez, Tommy, sometimes I forget how pretty this little swimmer's butt of yours is."

I felt him shimmy up between my spread legs, and grab me by the hip-bones so he could my position my rearend the way he liked it. My own boner was already throbbing. Then there was his cock sliding up and down my asscrack, which he liked to do to get us both heated up. He lubed my hole and his dick with some spit, and then set that hot, round dickhead against my buttslit.

"Take it easy, man," I said, "There hasn't been anything up there since you and Bobby fucked me back in September."

"Ohhhhh." he groaned as he ground the crown of his cock inside me and I let out a little squeal, "Tommy, you've got the hottest hole in the whole world. My dick still feels better when its up your butthole than anywhere else."

"AAhhhh!"

My asslips spasmed hard around that big ball on a stick for a minute, like they do the first fuck of every summer, like they have to remember what its like to have something coming in instead of going out. But then, Billy gave a push, and he went in a little more, and then another--"Ooohhhh!--and that pole of his slid right up me.

That cousin of mine really did have an amazing cock. That curve in it made it go places and do things I don't think dicks were ever meant to. I just closed my eyes and gave myself over to the pleasure of an old-fashioned asshole busting as Billy started pumping his meat in and out of me.

"Oh, yeah. Fuck me, Billy. Do it. Ohhh!"

"Oh, yeah. Take my fucking dick, Tommy. Oh, boy. That's it. Jeez, there's nothing like a hot man's asshole like yours to make a dick feel good."

We were rutting like a pair of happy hounds. God, did Billy know how to fuck! He had me squealing like a piece of pork, my hole was so glad, and I knew it would go and on. Billy was a master at the delay shot. Other summers, Bobby'd give me a hot five-minute ram-job that would leave my butthole throbbing, then Billy'd slide up my aching pucker and just keep it up and keep it up till I thought maybe he planned to fuck me forever.

"Jeez, Billy. It feels so good. There. Right there!"

"That the spot, Tommy? Oh, you love your cousin's big dick poking your hole, don't you? This pretty ass of yours was just made to take my dick up there."

"Oh, yeah. Fuck him, Billy. Fuck him real good!"

What?

I don't know exactly how long they'd been standing there. I just opened my eyes and there they were about six feet away--Bobby and Billy Junior. I freaked when I first saw them. I started to pull away from Billy, but he grabbed me around the chest and pushed his pole extra far up my ass and put his head up next to mine.

"You're not going anyplace, Tommy," he said, "You just stick your fanny up and keep on making my dick feel nice. Yeah."

Then, I noticed that Bobby had his cock out of his pants and was wanging away on it like crazy. But that wasn't all. Billy Junior had his fly open, and out of that flaming red bush of his, there was a prong that looked just like his Dad's at full staff. So he had inherited something from Billy after all. But what could that boy be thinking, watching his old man plunge his stiff babymaker--the very one that made Billy Junior--up his Uncle Tommy's hairy ass?

Billy started his long-dicking action--pulling his cock all the way out of my hole and then jamming it all the way back in, which always about made me go crazy. That curvy dick was just all over my guts, and having that cock head popping in and out and in and out of my buttlips just sent me into orbit. I was squalling like a hungry calf I wanted it so much.

It was then I heard Billy Junior:

"Oh, yeah, Dad. Fuck him hard. Fuck his ass hard! Yeah!"

Billy must have heard his boy talking, too, and it must have really turned him on, because I don't think in twenty years he'd battered my bunghole like he did then. Ram! Ram! Ram! That big prong of his was splitting my ass in half, like he was using my butt to show his boy just exactly what fucking was all about.

That hard, deep screwing just made me helpless. I wasn't even beating off, my boner slapping against my stomach each time Billy thrust. I didn't care about my dick right then, just about that special pleasure a man gets when his ass gets royally fucked. I spread my knees so far apart I thought I'd get a rupture so my hole was wide open to take every inch of Billy's steely manhood as deep inside as I could.

"Ohhh! Jeez! AHHH!" Billy started to shoot, spraying his juice up my guts. "AHHH!"

"Yeah, Dad. Yeah! Blow it up there. Yeah!"

"Give it to him, Billy."

"Ahhh! Ahhhh!" Billy kept pumping his gyzm up my butthole. The sweat dripped down from his face onto my back and shoulders. My sphincter was grabbing at his dick like crazy, and I all of a sudden could feel the bursting, throbbing ache of my own raging hardon.

"Ahhh! Whew! Yeah!" Billy collapsed over me and gave me a bearhug. "Whoo-whee!" He slapped me hard on one asscheek, "Tommy, you got the hottest hole God ever created." I felt him straighten up and start to pull his still hard dick out. "Bobby, I think this man's butt could use some more fucking."

"Naw, not yet," Bobby said, "Hell, I think we better let the boy go next or he'll pop before he gets a chance."

I looked behind me. At some point, Billy Junior'd moved around to get a different angle on the action. I thought vaguely about what it must have been like for him standing there, watching how his old man fucked: seeing his Dad's ass pump up and down, catching a glimpse of his old man's puckerhole as Billy's cheeks opened and closed when he was ploughing me really hard, until those hairy buns grabbed and dimpled as Billy planted a big load of Billy Junior seeds way deep inside me. And finally, seeing his old man's big-headed, curving boner--a twin to Billy Junior's own--slick with gyzm and assjuice when he pulled it out of my hole.

But right then, all Billy Junior was looking at was his Uncle Tommy's furry, spread fanny, smiling up at him like an invitation, stretched out and begging. Somewhere along the line, he'd pulled his shirt off and dropped his pants down around his boot-tops, that dick sticking out in front of him like a flagpole. That boy was a sight to behold, all hairless on his chest, with that bush that looked like somebody'd set his crotch on fire, it was so red. He looked a little nervous. Then again, I figured he'd probably never fucked an asshole before, and I'm sure he never expected to ream the one between the cheeks of his thirty-nine year old uncle, especially with his own Dad and his Uncle Bobby looking on.

"Go ahead, boy," Billy said. "If you get something wrong, your Uncle Tommy'll let you know."

"Yeah," Bobby said. "Just look how he bad he wants that big peter of yours."

I was kind of wiggling my butt back and forth, as if to show him it was all right. I know it's weird, but the notion of Billy Junior fucking me there in front of Billy and Bobby was really turning me on. He was almost exactly the same age as his father had been the first time he reamed me out, and even if the rest of him didn't look a thing like Billy, that boy's dick was a carbon copy. With his stick up me, it would be just like twenty years ago, when Bobby'd opened my hole and then Billy'd taken over and I'd learned how good getting fucked could feel. The only difference was that, this time, it would be like it was Billy who'd taken my cherry instead of his brother, and it was his own son coming up for sloppy seconds.

"Shit! Get with it, Billy Junior!" Billy barked.

Billy Junior got down behind me and put that prize cockhead of his against my buttlips and gave a little push. Nothing happened. Then I felt his hand down there kind of readjusting things--his thumb and forefinger pulling me open just a little and the warm tip of his dick on my pink hole. Then he pushed again, and that dick just spread by begging pucker and slid in easy as pie. His old man had loosened me up pretty good, raking around this way and that, and my asshole had an extra load of lube from the big wad of come Billy'd left up there. Billy Junior started to go to it, kind of tentative at first. He made real shallow thrusts, as if he was kind of scared of what he was doing. But then he began to pump a little harder, and to move it around a little up my hole.

I groaned. "Ohhhh. Yeah, boy. You got it. Oh, wow..."

"That's it, son. Make him happy."

"Oh, yeah. Yeah, Uncle Tommy. Oh, it feels real good, Uncle

Tommy!

"Do it, boy. That's it."

"Fuck him, Billy Junior," Bobby laughed, "Show your old man here you can teach him a thing or two. Yeah!"

It kind of surprised me. Billy Junior went at it like a pro, like even if he'd never had his dick up an ass, he knew a thing or two when it came to buttfucking. He didn't have his father's technique, but hell, he's just a kid nineteen. And I think his whole shaft might have even been a little thicker than his Dad's. He reamed my pucker out real respectably, getting that teenage dick in as far as it would go and then roiling it around and stirring up my guts real good, then pulling way back and kind of teasing my inside buttlips with the crown of his pecker. He even tried out some of that long-dicking action he'd seen his old man use to drive me crazy.

"That's it, son. Yeah! That's it. That's what he likes."

Billy was a regular cheering section for that boy. Of course, I guess it makes sense. I mean, here's that little bottom you diapered and wiped and spanked, all grown up and rippling and ramming back and forth. And here's that little peter you remember him peeing with that's as big as yours and hard as stone. And here that boy is, ploughing up the same hot butthole you've been fucking for twenty years. Shit, of course he going to be proud.

"Slam it up there, Billy Junior! Hard! You got to fuck a man hard! That's no pussy, that's an asshole! Ram it in! That's it! Yeah!"

Billy Junior's longdicking didn't last long. It must've felt so good on his cock he couldn't stand it. He suddenly shoved his throbber way in and started that final pumping.

"Ahhh! Ohhhh! AHHHH! AHHHH!"

He gave me a real good flood up the gut. It felt like a fucking pint of boyjuice mixing up there with his old man's spunk. He leaned down over me as the last bit of his load dribbled out, and whispered to me, "Thanks, Uncle Tommy. Thanks."

After Billy Junior shot, it was Bobby's turn. He didn't even last as long up my tail as the boy did. I think watching both his brother and his nephew fuck my ass had almost been too much for him. But that cone-shaped dick of his did give me a chance to blow my load. Lord, the base of his fuckstick is thick, and how old Bobby loves to have it jammed all the way up me, racheting it back and forth! I think that man must pump his pud all year dreaming of my butthole that's going to beg for his massive pole. His pubes were rasping against my butthairs and his little paunch was kind of tickling my cheeks and my hand went to work on my own boner, and my buttlips bore down on Bobby's fat pussyreamer and Blam!, I started to spatter all over the fucking camp-site, with both Billy and Billy Junior urging me on.

"Oh, yeah, come one, Tommy. Shoot. Shoot your big load! Show Bobby how you like it! Shoot that load!"

"Do it, Uncle Tommy! Come on! Show me how you come off! Do it! Yeah!"

"AHHHH!"

"AHHHH!"

Both Bobby and I blasted almost simultaneously. He was still pump-ing juice up my butt when I just collapsed on the ground, I was so exhausted. Billy pulled out and the gyz of my two cousins and that "nephew" of mine just sort of drooled out of my asshole. It really burned back there, but, boy, I was happy.

This wasn't going to be such a bad trip after all.

Later, we all had a long talk. Billy really didn't know what to say to Billy Junior when he wanted to come along, but finally figured there was no way he couldn't bring him. As they drove up in the car, he told the boy how long the three of us cousins had been doing this, and that, when we got together, there were some sort of man things we did that maybe he wouldn't expect. Billy Junior said it was all so vague and kind of embarrassed he didn't know what the hell was going on.

So then, on the trail, Billy and Bobby have a long talk, and Bobby says to his brother that he's a stupid dick for not telling the kid outright what the score is if he 's going to bring him along in the first place. So, when Bobby and Billy Junior go off that morning, old Uncle Bobby set the boy straight in about three minutes.

"You remember, Billy Junior? You should have seen the look on his face. I ask if he knows what Billy was talking about, that 'man things' crap, and he says that well, no, he didn't quite get it. So I just come right out and say to him that when we go camping his dad and me always fuck his Uncle Tommy up the asshole, that we've been doing it for twenty years. I tell him that the rest of the year, none of us messes around or anything, but that, come summertime, it's just another one of those things that we do when we get together. 'About now,' I say to the boy--you remember? 'About now, I bet, your old man's already pumping his dick up your Uncle Tommy's hairy little butt.'" Bobby laughed. "But then...Then! Billy Junior just stops dead and looks at me and he says, "'Well, maybe we better get back there.'"

The story's making the boy blush. We're all laughing about it. The Wild Turkey makes another round.

But finally, it's a little late, and I stretch and say, "I don't know about you guys, but I got me one hell of a sore asshole, and I'm going to hit the hay."

It is sore, too. I took all three of them on again around two o'clock. And then the boy wanted some more around sunset, so I took him over to the edge of the campsite and dropped my pants while Billy and Bobby got dinner ready--bitching and moaning and every so often coming over to beat off a little and give the boy some pointers on his ass-fucking technique.

"Yeah. I think that's about what we're all ready for," Billy says, his face flushed. "Right, boy?"

Billy Junior yawns. "Right, Dad."

IV.

I don't know what time it is. There's somebody shaking my shoulder. The night's chilly, and I pull my sleeping bag closer around me. The shaking goes on.

I open my eyes. It's Billy Junior. He's out of his own bag, with his sweat clothes on. He puts his fingers to his lips, and signals for me to follow him.

Shit. A nineteen year old pecker doesn't give you any rest.

But what the hell. I get up, and already I've got a hardon tenting out my own sweatpants. Billy and Bobby finally stayed up a little later to tell some more jokes and kill the Wild Turkey. They're snoring like the Second Coming itself wouldn't wake them.

I put on some shoes, and then Billy Junior takes me by the arm and, without a word, guides me through the woods. I don't know where the hell we're headed, but in about five minutes, there's a pond I remember seeing on some other trip, another one of those places where Bobby likes to fish. It was probably about to here that they got before Bobby spilled the beans about everything and they decided to turn back.

There's a bright, waning moon out, so I can see everything real clear. Billy Junior's still holding onto my arm.

"Uncle Tommy," he says softly, "Uncle Tommy, you know, I really think it's great that you guys let me come along, and it's really important to me that you've all been doing this for so long, and it's not that I don't like fucking your ass and all. I'd never fucked a guy before. But, well, see, there's three or four seniors on the rugby team, and me and them... Well, we kind of play around, too, but... Well, see, it's always them that ... Ah, shit!..."

Suddenly, he breaks away and steps away a couple paces. He stands there in the moonlight and kicks off his shoes. Then he pulls his pants off so he's just got his sweatshirt on. His butt and legs shimmer white in the light, like marble.

He leans over and bends his knees. The moon's bright enough that I can see almost everything there is too see about redheaded, teenager's ass. It's not hairy like mine or Bobby's or his old man's. It's smooth as glass, except maybe just a little tuft of fur there at the deepest part of that crack of his stuck-out butt.

"Please, Uncle Tommy. Don't say anything to Dad or Uncle Bobby," he says.

Then he reaches around with both hands and pulls those tight buns wide apart. He bends over even farther so his ass pokes way up in the air.

"This is the way they make me get when they do it to me."

I step up behind him and drop my sweatpants to my knees. My dick is as stiff as its ever been in my life. I think back over those twenty years...

Maybe this is the beginning of a whole new tradition.

"Oh, please, Uncle Tommy," Billy Junior says urgently. " Fuck me. Fuck me!"

OFF THE MENU
by Barry Alexander

Jess stuck her head around the door of my office. "He's back! Table 8."

I looked up from the ad copy I was proofing and tried to glare at my assistant manager. It was hard. Jess had an infectious grin and I had to tighten my lips to keep from answering. Even her tightly frizzled red hair looked perky. "Damn it, Jess, you know I'm not in on Fridays. Go away and let me get some work done."

The smile on her face fell. "OK, OK. Just thought you'd want to know."

She walked away and left me feeling guilty for snapping at her. She was trying to help after all. For the hundredth time, I regretted letting her know I was gay. Of course, I didn't have much choice after she caught me kissing my now ex-boyfriend. At least she finally stopped trying to fix me up with single women.

My reprieve didn't last long. When I started working on my day off to keep my mind off my break-up, Jess quickly realized what had happened.. She adjusted her ideas of what constituted my ideal mate and started to point out every good-looking man who walked into my restaurant, in spite of my protests that I was not looking to start a new relationship. Ever since her engagement, Jess seemed to think it her duty to trap everyone else in the bonds of holy matrimony. She was convinced her woman's intuition gave her a special kind of gaydar.

I thought we'd settled things. I'd had a nice little chat with her after the last guy she pointed out. The guy sitting alone had been handsome. I was toying with the idea of introducing myself, when the man's wife and two daughters came out of the restroom to join him.

"But they're not happy together -- I can see it." Jess had said when I mentioned her little oversight.

"If an unhappy marriage was all it took to make a man gay, seventy-five percent of the men in this country would be gay."

"But you need to start dating again. It's been six months since you split up. You've got to at least try asking out some of these guys."

"I'm doing just fine. I don't need another man in my life right now. I appreciate your concern. Really. But face it, Jess. Straight women don't have gaydar." Jess just smiled.

I tried to go back to work. But all I could see was the gorgeous man who'd come in for lunch every day this week. With a different guy each time, I reminded myself. I did not need another guy like my ex. Even if this man's skin was the dark warm brown of rich maple syrup. So what if he hid the body of a god under his expensive suits -- all hard muscles and animal strength? I couldn't care less; I had work to do.

I walked through the restaurant and headed for the kitchen. I was thirsty. I needed something to drink. I was not checking out the man at table 8. There was absolutely no reason for Jess to walk past and wink at me.

Richard Johnson (OK, so I'd checked on his name -- it's important to know a customer's name) was even better looking than I'd remembered. Damn, but he was fine! His current lunch companion was not up to his usual standards. The guy looked like he bought the kind of suits that came with a reversible jacket and two pairs of pants. He was also clearly nervous, not that I blamed him. Sitting next to a god had to be distracting.

Richard -- I could not imagine anyone having the gall to call him Dick -- made some comment and waited while his guest industriously masticated an overlarge mouthful of Chicken Marseilles. When he tried to gulp it down so he that could reply, he choked. As Richard leaned over to help, the klutz grabbed for his water goblet and somehow dumped it down Richard's pristine white shirt. That shirt probably cost more than the other guy's suit, but Richard never even complained. He was very solicitous, patting the guy on the back and offering him his own water. He brushed off the red-faced apologies his lunch companion proffered.

While the waiter was mopping up the table, Richard opened his jacket and tried to dry himself. It was no use; the front of his shirt was drenched. The nearly-transparent white fabric clung to his chest and stomach revealing every ripple. The icy water had perked his nipples, the dark points thrusting against the wet cloth. He excused himself from the table.

I suddenly felt an intense need to wash my hands. I walked into the restroom and my jaw gaped open. I knew the guy was hot, but I hadn't expected anything like the vision that greeted me. Bare-chested, he stood in front of the hand dryer, holding his wet shirt under the hot air.

He turned to look at me when the door swung open. Muscles rippled under mahogany skin. His nipples protruded like dark chocolates kisses and I wanted to rain kisses over his body. He was magnificent. A man like that shouldn't have to hide all that perfection under a corporate suit. A man like that should be stretched out naked on my bed where I could truly appreciate his fine qualities.

He grinned at me. "Damned clumsy fool. Glad it was just mineral water." But there was no rancor in his tone. "Employees can be such a pain." His deep voice rumbled sending vibrations straight to my cock.

" Uh -- tell me about it." Brilliant repartee. That would really interest him. Then I realized what he'd said -- his dinner companions were only employees. All right! He was not a better looking version of my ex boyfriend.

"I'm beginning to think taking everyone to lunch was not the best way to get to know my new staff. I thought I'd show them I don't bite." He laughed, a warm rich chuckle. "But this guy is going to take some convincing."

I tried to keep my eyes front and center, after all there was plenty to look at -- broad shoulders, nice pecs, rippled stomach -- but I failed.

My eyes drifted down the massive column of his throat, down to the deep valley between his pecs, down to his lickable nipples, down to the smooth ripples of his stomach, down and down and down. My eyes locked on the front of his expensive trousers and stayed there. His basket wasn't prominent in the finely cut slacks, but there was definitely something nice there. I thought I saw a slight shifting of contents and felt an answering twitch in my own dick.

He caught me looking. His eyes flashed and I flushed. The guy could be straight, and I was practically coming on to him. I walked over to the sink to wash my hands. As I bent over the sink, I could feel the flush creeping up the back of neck. But more intensely, I could feel his eyes on me. I suddenly understood his lunch companion's confusion - - I couldn't think of a decent response to save my life. I didn't know if he was angry or checking me out. My tight slacks did frame the small rounds of my ass nicely. I couldn't afford to anger a customer who came in every day and ordered from the most expensive items on the menu. If we hadn't been in my own restaurant, I might have risked returning that look. I didn't dare. I scrubbed my hands briefly under the other hand dryer and went back to my office. He didn't say a word, but I could still feel his eyes watching me.

I didn't get a hell of a lot of work done that afternoon.

Jess came back right before the end of her shift. "Sorry to interrupt, but that guy is back. He insists on seeing you, but he won't say why. I tried telling him you weren't in, but he says he knows you're here."

I sighed. "What guy? Well, don't worry about it, Jess," I said before she could answer. "I'll take care of it."

"Do you need me for anything else? I was just ready to go off shift, but I can stay if you want."

I looked up at her in surprise. Jess had an odd look in her eyes. I'd probably find out about it tomorrow, whatever it was.

"No, go on home, Jess. I'll take care of it. Probably some jerk trying to sell something or get a free meal. Show him in."

I was still studying reports when I heard him enter the office. "I'll be with you in a second." It never hurts to give the impression of being swamped with work.

My door shut with a thud and I looked up. Oh my god, it was him. The black god from lunch. Richard Johnson leaned against my door, arms folded across his chest. He scowled at me.

I was suddenly aware of just how big he was. Six foot four of prime man. And my eyes started to wander down his torso again. Hastily, I jerked them back to his face. I was startled by intensity in his dark eyes. "Is there a problem?"

"I saw the way you were looking at me today. I thought you were just another diner until I saw you walk into the back," he said softly in the sexiest voice I had ever heard.

"Ah, look, I'm sorry. I didn't realize I was staring. I was just surprised to see someone half-naked in the restroom."

His face broke out into a big grin. "I was hoping you'd want to do a little more than look." His dark eyes flashed with desire. Then he turned around and flipped the lock on the door, and smiled.

I looked at him and I suddenly didn't give a damn how many guys he had slept with, just as long as I was one of them. But I was at work. What if someone heard us?

I stood up and walked towards him, intending to invite him home. I looked up into those warm dark eyes, and suddenly couldn't frame a coherent sentence.

"I think I'm going to have to do something about that," he said softly. "I'd better teach you what happens to men who look at me like that."

I wanted to answer, but I all I could do was stare helplessly at him. I could almost feel the heat radiating off that body. And I could smell the sweet mixture of some exotic aftershave and hard male body. Later, I told myself. Now, my cock insisted, hardening and squirming in my briefs as it sought escape.

"Now that's the kind of thing I mean," he said with a smile, his eyes aimed at my erring crotch.

Then he took a step closer. I could feel the heat from his body. A quiver ran through me. I was in serious trouble. I couldn't think of a single excuse to delay what was going to happen. I should not be doing this here. I didn't want everyone in the restaurant hearing the sounds of our lovemaking. I should invite him back to my place. I should --

I stood frozen helplessly as he pulled me to him. Then his mouth came down hard on mine, his lips locked over mine, and his wet tongue forced my lips apart and plunged inside.

After the first touch of his lips, I forgot all about anyone who might overhear us. I just knew I had to have him and now. The man was hot. I pressed my body against his, feeling the strong, steady beat of his heart against my chest. I sucked on his tongue like it was a slice of ripe peach, smooth and sweet and succulent.

His hands moved over my back and one slipped down inside my slacks and under my briefs, cupping one cheek in his palm. He pulled me closer, and I felt the hard tube of his cock against my belly, its heat radiating through my shirt. His fingers dug into my cheek as he held me against him. This close, the scent of hot man was intoxicating.

I opened a couple buttons so I could slide my hand inside, and explore his massive chest. I found one of his nipples and tweaked it. He grunted in response, and slid a finger down my crevice. I groaned when the tip of his finger brushed gently against my hole. I waited for more, but he pulled his hand free. I would have protested, but my mouth was still occupied. His tongue rolled over my mine and plunged down my throat. Just when I thought I couldn't breath anymore, he came up for air.

He grinned at me. I couldn't help staring at the mouth that had just plundered mine. His lips were full, and the color of dark sweet cherries, and I started fantasizing about all the places I wanted those lips to explore.

"Why don't you get out of those clothes so I can give you what we both know you want."

I felt a little awkward undressing when he was still fully clothed. My body is pretty average, everything there but nothing outstanding. But he watched me strip as eagerly as if I was some kind of model. It was erotic having such an appreciate audience. I couldn't resist showing off my best feature. When I slid out of my slacks, I turned around and gave him the full view of the butt he was going to be filling. My butt is fairly small, but the cheeks are hard and round. I bent over to take off my shoes so I could remove my pants. I knew I was flashing my hole and I lingered over my laces, so he could get a good look at my dark rose.

Then I felt a stinging slap across my hole. I yelped.

"You ought not to be flashing that thing, until I get undressed."

His basket had really swollen, and I wanted to drop to my knees right there and check him out. But as soon as his hand reached for his shirt buttons, I knew I'd have to wait. I had to see the whole package..

I glanced frantically around the office for something to fuck on. Not even a leather couch. Everything streamlined and functional. At the time I bought it, I'd thought my chrome and glass desk gave a touch of class to the office. I looked at the delicate legs and knew it wouldn't hold us. I could just hear it crashing and imagined my waiters break-ing the door down to see if I was all right.

Then he took off his shirt and I forgot about such mundane things as office furniture. His chest looked just as edible as it had in the restroom. Muscles rippled easily under his skin as he unbuttoned, unbuckled, and unzipped. A white jock strap bundled his cock and balls into an appealing package. The contrast made his skin look even darker and richer, the color of baker's chocolate.

The man had a body made to be worshipped. He looked like he was carved from ebony -- all sculpted curves and smooth planes. I wanted to spend a lifetime exploring his topography with my lips and tongue -- plateaus and peaks, valleys and forest, secret hollows and bold promontories.

He pulled down his jock strap and his dick sprang free, not overly long, but hard and thick just the way I liked them. He stepped gracefully out of his jock and tossed it casually aside. It landed on my jumbled pile of clothes. I grinned. I had a souvenir, but that was for later. Right now I had the real thing within reach.

His thick cock was shielded with a skin that looked like dark choco-late, forming a fluted ring around the rich raspberry crown. A drizzle of clear fluid trembled at the tip.

I wanted to stick my tongue inside that skin and sample that warm sweet berry. I loved chocolate-covered cherries -- the sweet drizzle of liquid center, the smooth firm cherry, the rich dark chocolate. His glossy pubes curled about the shaft , thick and dense like the tightly woven nap of an expensive Berber carpet.

His heavily weighted scrotum swayed gently like a pendulum beneath his cock as he walked towards me. He strode over to my desk and planted his naked butt on my oversized manager's chair. He swiveled the chair around to face me, and leaned forward, spreading his legs. "Get over here."

His low hangers puddled on the leather seat. He held his dick in one hand and slowly stroked it, his eyes never leaving mine. I knelt before him, unsure which treasure to explore first. . I hadn't felt this way about a man in a long time. I ran my hands up the sculptured pillars of his thighs, brushing my thumbs against the heavy pouch. So hot. He gave a little gasp and I leaned closer and swallowed one of his balls. I sucked on it gently, swirling my tongue over the surface. He fisted his cock slowly, while I slurped at his nuts. The movement of his fist on his cock jiggled his scrotum as I licked the back of his sac.

He tapped me on the nose with his cock, leaving a smear of precum on my cheek. He didn't have to ask twice. One look at that prime meat and I abandoned his balls to kiss the puckered ring just covering his glans.. Holding the shaft in one hand, I gently held the skin in place and tucked my tongue inside the silky membrane. He squirmed and gasped as I swiped my tongue over the glossy raspberry crown. He cupped the back of my head and gave me a firm push to show me just where he wanted that cock to go. I opened wider, and his cock coasted over my tongue and knocked at the back of my palate. I swallowed and it slid right down, in spite of its size. I really wanted that cock. He thrust his hips up at me, my chair squeaked rhythmically. My fingers skimmed over his muscular thighs and curved over the hard rounds of his ass. The man was solid everywhere I touched. My head bobbed between his thighs as I swallowed him. My jaw was getting tired but that big cock felt so good packing my throat I didn't want to quit.

He must have liked it too, because he was really squirming around in that chair. When he pushed me off, we were both breathing hard. I knelt between his legs and grinned up at him. A slow smile spread across his broad face. He reached out one hand and wiped the wet-ness from my mouth.

"Mmm, that was nice. Now stand up so I can see you."

I kept my eyes locked on his as I stood up. He leaned back in my chair, arms behind his head, moist tufts of hair shadowed his pits. He looked me over, ignoring his spit-shiny cock that bobbed between us. I waited for his verdict.

"Niiiiiice," he said, drawling out the word. He sat up and wrapped his hand around my cock. My cock looked dwarfed by his big hand, but his touch was gentle. His other hand cradled my balls, cupping them as gently as if he were holding a newborn kitten. I trembled between his hands.

"So sweet, baby," he crooned in that deep voice that sank right down to my balls. "Let me look at all of you. Let me see that pretty little hole."

I felt like a slut but I turned around and spread my legs apart, brac-ing my hands on the glass desk. I heard the chair squeak as he leaned forward. "Mmm, mmm, mmm, that's a damn fine ass, man. And I'm going to treat it right."

My asscheeks quivered as he slowly stroked them. Then he bent down and ran his tongue along the sweaty crevice. I jumped. He steadied me with his hands as his tongue ran laps around my puckered ring.

I'd been afraid someone would hear, but when his tongue touched me, I didn't give a damn who heard my moans. I was incoherent with lust as his hot tongue flickered over me. I spread my legs wider, inviting him in. My hole fluttered open. He laughed, his breath tickling my cheeks. His hands continued to stroke me but he started teasing me with his thumb, rubbing it around the sensitive opening, and tapping it on the hole until I was whimpering with frustration.

"What do you want?" he asked softly.

I couldn't think of anything I wanted more right then than to have that big cock filling the emptiness inside me. I pushed back against him, trying to suck in his teasing finger at least.

" No, you have to tell me first."

"I want it, damn it. Give me that big hard dick. Shove it inside me."

"Now that wasn't so hard was it." He put his hands on my hips and swung me around. "Man, you should have seen that hole of yours: it just opened wide and said come on in. We just need a couple more things."

"Top left drawer, in the staple box."

He dumped the box on the desk. He handed me the lube and opened a condom. The discarded package fluttered to the floor like a white butterfly. "Extra-large. You must have know I was coming."

His cock stuck straight up out of his lap, as he rolled the latex over it. He grinned lewdly at me. "Bet it's been a long time since you got stuffed with this much meat Why don't you just get up here and we'll see how much of it you can take?"

I squeezed some lube onto my dick and worked a generous amount inside me. I was going to need all the help I could get taking that monster. I climbed into the chair, my knees beside his thighs, and my butt poised over his cock. He centered that big dick on my bull's eye and started to push. He was so big he stretched me wide open as he filled me slowly with cock -- inch after inch after inch. Pain pricked at my eyelids, but in a few seconds I opened to him and he slid more easily inside. I thought he was never going to hit bottom. Then he gave a little groan as his groin snugged against my ass.

"Oh, yeah , " he sighed. "I think I'm just going to let it soak up all this heat. You're so hot."

I could feel the little tremors running through his cock as he tried to hold it still. I clamped down on him and was amazed again at how thick he was. He jumped a little when I squeezed so I did it again. I ground my butt against his groin. I didn't mind working for it. His cock rubbed against the sides of my passage every time I moved. Each bump sending a new tingle of pleasure down my spine. I ground and squeezed and pushed back at him, but the damn fool wouldn't move. He just kept that big dick plugged up my butt. I needed more. He had me whining with frustration.

"Come on, what are you waiting for? Fuck me!"

"You want it?"

"Damn right. Fuck me, damn it."

"All I wanted to hear."

He half- lifted me out of his lap. His cock slid out of me with a rush and my guts collapsed on the sudden emptiness. He pulled almost out, holding me off him with his strength. I started to protest, then he said, "Hold on, I'm coming in."

He let go and I slid back down his cock, taking half of it back in. He grabbed my hips and rammed that big fucker up me. I squealed when it slid past my prostrate. Then I felt his wiry bush scraping my cheeks and sighed with contentment. The man felt so good up there.

I hung onto his shoulders and fucked myself on his big pole. Every time I came down, he slammed his hips up, punching me good. He pulled me to him and our mouths locked together, his tongue thrusting and fucking my mouth as fiercely as his cock surge inside me.

He fisted my cock, as I humped against him, riding him as hard as I could. His cock kept nudging my prostrate, sending sparks of pleasure up my spine. I tried to hold it off, to let the feelings build, stronger, higher, to some impossible peak I had never reached before. But it was so damned good! And when his mouth moved down my chest and he started tongue lashing my nipple, I knew I was lost. My balls were clamped tightly to my dick, and I was dripping precum all over my belly. When he took one of my hard nipples between his teeth and bit, fire raced up my spine. I gasped against his neck and my guts spasmed around his cock. The first jet hit him right on the chin. Others drizzled down his chest and stomach, the thick white ropes like marbling against his dark skin.

I was still shooting, when he grabbed my hips and held me in place. His hips rabbit-fucked me as he groaned and gasped and rocketed a pay load inside me. I collapsed against him, my heart hammering in my chest, my body still trembling from the force of orgasm. A final shudder passed through his body, like the after tremors of an earthquake.

He let go of me, and reluctantly I sat up, not eager to break our connection.

He smiled at me. "I was getting bored with your menu. But now I know what you have off the menu, I think I'll have to come back."

"Anytime. No reservations necessary."

"How did things work out?" Jess asked worriedly, when she came in the next day. "The man seemed so upset."

"Well, I think I managed to calm him down some. He seemed quite satisfied when he left."

"You're so good with handling customers. I just wish you could do as well with finding a boyfriend."

I managed to keep my face impassive until. she turned to go. I suppose I should have told her she was right about this one, but I'd be damned if I was going to admit some straight woman had better gaydar than me. She'd never let me forget it.

DON'T ASK, DON'T TELL
by David Laurents

"What do you think of it?"

Eddie stared up at the tank in transparent awe. "It's...it's huge."

Luke grinned. "Wait'll you see what I've got to show you inside."

Eddie blushed, his pale, beautiful face turning all rosy as he nervously looked behind him to make sure no one had heard Luke's double entendre. He tried to make the action seem casual by running his hands along the tank's hull, but it was painfully obvious that this was an afterthought. Luke sighed. What am I doing getting involved with someone so green, he wondered, so...young. But damn, he was cute. Luke worked out as often as possible, but try as he might, he spent far too much time sitting at the controls of the tank to ever manage a body like Eddie's, built from training and hard work out in the sun. But that didn't stop him from wanting to experience a body like that second hand. Or, more literally, by hand...

"Come on," Luke said, climbing onto the rungs leading to the hatch. "You're never going to believe what's inside."

Eddie took a last nervous look around, then hurried up and into the tank. A smile broke out on Luke's face when Eddie gasped as he descended into the control cabin. It was a common reaction, akin to visiting New York City for the first time. A bank of screens gave a three sixty view of their surroundings, while AC chased away the wet jungle heat.

Eddie ran his hand along the plush fabric of the seats, then stood in front of the screens, gawking at the view like a tourist.

"Impressive, isn't it?" Luke asked, stepping up behind Eddie and wrapping his arms around him. Eddie stiffened, evidently alarmed, and

tried to step out from Luke's grasp. "Shh, it's all right. They're not windows, they're monitors. Did you see any windows on the outside?"
Eddie paused his struggling, letting this new information sink in, then
relaxed into Luke's embrace. Luke ran his hands down Eddie's chest,
nuzzled at his ear. After a moment, Eddie turned around to face him,
to tentatively return his kisses and explorations.

Luke sat on one of the command chairs and pulled Eddie into his lap.
They kissed and groped again, Luke slowly guiding Eddie along with
gentle direction. Eddie wasn't all that green, Luke discovered, or if he
was he faked it well as he met Luke's passion with equal intensity, and
grew bolder in his explorations, reaching down to fondle Luke through
the fabric of his camouflage pants. Luke tilted his head back, reveling
in the feel of Eddie's hand along his cock, the rub of the fabric. He
longed for Eddie to unzip him, to pull his cock out from these clinging
green fabric and lock his lips around it instead. But there would be time
for that. He didn't want to rush Eddie, who idly let his hands wander
back up Luke's chest to tweak his nipples.

Luke opened his eyes again and smiled at him. He tugged Eddie's
unbuttoned shirt from his pants and ran his tongue up and down
Eddie's hard, chiseled chest, exploring all the planes of its surface, the
salt taste of his skin.

"Watch this," Luke said, after a moment, smiling. "Put the chair
back, Peter," he called aloud. Slowly, the back of the chair flattened
into a bed. "Thanks, Peter," Luke mumbled absently, running his
tongue around Eddie's left nipple.

"You're welcome, Luke."

Suddenly, Eddie jerked away from him, rolling onto the floor.

"What?" Luke asked, wondering again why he was getting involved
with someone so young. So he doesn't like his nipples bit, Luke told
himself. OK, I can live with that. He could have just told me so, more
simply.

"Who the hell was that?" Eddie demanded, and suddenly Luke knew
what was the matter.

He smiled, and sat up, facing Eddie where he struggled to put his shirt back on. "It's just the computer." He reached forward for Eddie, to gently interfere with his putting on his shirt again by holding him, caressing him.

But Eddie drew back, still clutching his shirt around him. "It sounded like a person. Is there someone else in here? Is someone watching?"

Luke sighed, and thought of his erection in his pants, realizing he would have to slow down a whole lot if he ever wanted it taken care of. "It's supposed to sound like a person," he explained. "It's an AI, an Artificial Intelligence. It's programmed to think like a person." Eddie looked about to protest again, but Luke didn't give him the chance. "But it isn't. I call him Peter because it's quicker than his code, PTR25. More personal. I spend a lot of time alone in here, talking to the computer, and it helps me feel like I'm not talking to myself. But he is just a computer, not a person. We're alone in here, just the two of us."

Eddie looked still unconvinced. "Can't it turn us in? I mean, won't it have records of us being in here or something?"

Luke sighed and reminded himself to go slow, gently. "I was going to do this later, but if it'll make you more comfortable we can take care of it now. Peter, you are not to register anything about Edward McDonnell. Erase every trace of him from your records: voice, image, the works. Also, I want you to erase the fact that I ever gave you this order. But, I want you to keep the order in effect, just hidden so that it can't be traced. I have a feeling," Luke said, smiling at Eddie and running his hands through Eddie's short blond hair, "he's going to be coming here often."

Eddie looked around the tank, as if searching for some evidence that the command had taken effect. Luke smiled at him, gentle and reassuring, waiting for Eddie to resume their lovemaking.

"As you ordered, Luke," Peter said.

Eddie relaxed visibly and stopped clutching his shirt around him. It fell to the ground again, revealing his magnificent chest, still wet in places from Luke's tongue. "Happy now?" Luke asked, and Eddie smiled and nodded. "Good, now get back up here."

Eddie laughed out loud, his voice ringing out solidly to fill the cabin. "As you ordered, Luke," he said, and climbed back into Luke's lap.

###

Luke watched from the hatch as Eddie hurried away from the tank, making a beeline for the mess hall before doubling back towards the barracks. He sighed at Eddie's obvious attempts at subterfuge and wished, not for the first time, that he could talk to the AI about this as he climbed back down into the control cabin and lounged, naked, in the command chair. But he knew not to. The AI was programmed with military regulations, which forbade homosexuality. Since Peter had no record of Eddie ever being there, they were safe, but if he spoke openly to Peter, the computer would be forced to turn them in when it filed its next field report.

And anyway, while Peter could respond to questions and directives, even analyze military strategy and learn from its own mistakes, the computer thought too literally to understand human relationships, to understand desire, trust, love, mistakes.

So, Luke kept his thoughts to himself, musing in silence late into the night, and many nights to come. And, for the next three weeks, until he was sent South into combat, he and Eddie conducted their brief but tumultuous affair in secret within the control cabin of the tank.

###

Luke glanced at the time-display on the control panel again, then back at the sensor displays showing the tank's surroundings. He had hoped Eddie would come say goodbye to him that night, that they would make love one last time before he went into combat, in case he might never return. But it seemed he was wrong. He cursed himself for being such a sentimental fool, felt angry to find he was blinking back tears as he stared at the barracks, waiting that one last moment, hoping against hope, to see Eddie running towards him and Peter. Eddie's beautiful face swam in front of his vision, the sharp lines of his body, the gentle curve of his cock as it arched towards Eddie's belly when erect.

Luke shook his head, to try and clear the image, but it was no use. He couldn't get the boy out of his mind, and all the scenes of their love-making came flooding back to him: the awkward and touching first night, as they explored each others bodies and grew used to them, learning what most turned each other on; the quickies they had when Eddie was off duty for half an hour, and came to find him in the tank; times they spent just being intimate, touching, holding, kissing; sometimes Eddie came and with hardly a word dropped down on his knees to unzip Luke's pants and take his cock into his mouth, as if he were desperately starving for it; the first time they had anal sex, Eddie's first time ever, and the welcoming way he trusted Luke, lying back on the command chair and spreading his legs wide and inviting... All these images came back into Luke's mind in a rushing flood, like the way they said a man's life passed suddenly before his eyes in the moments before he knew he was about to die.

Luke had grown hard as a rock thinking of Eddie, and he wished Eddie had come to say goodbye even if they hadn't fucked farewell. There had been more to their relationship than just the sex, damnit.

But he couldn't wait any longer. He had his orders, had to be at the new site by 04:00. "Roll on out," he told Peter, then settled down in his chair to sulk.

###

Eddie jerked to his feet when he heard the engines rev. He'd been sitting with his back against the tank's hull, waiting for Luke to return. He had spent half an hour banging on the hull, climbing up to the hatch to see if he could slip inside and surprise Luke when he came back, lying naked on the command chair, waiting for him, but the tank was impenetrable. After a while, Eddie gave up banging lest someone over-hear him and wonder why he was attacking the machine. He had set-tled down out of sight from the barracks to wait for Luke, so they could see each other one last time and say goodbye.

As he was waiting he kept thinking about Luke, wondering what he would do for the three weeks that Luke was in combat. He knew he would worry about him all the time, wondering if he was OK, worrying that something might have happened to him. He knew Peter was the latest in advanced tank design, he could tell just from the brain that computer had, but he worried it might not be enough protection to save Luke, if the combat got bad.

When the tank lurched forward, Eddie realized Luke was already inside, that he had been in there the entire time. Eddie leapt to his feet and dashed in front of it, jumping up and down and waving his hands, trying to get Luke's attention on the sensors. But Luke was ignoring him. He kept driving straight ahead as if Eddie did not exist. Eddie couldn't believe it. He felt a tearing pain inside his chest. Was this the same Luke he'd fallen in love with over these last few weeks? What had happened that Luke could so coldly ignore him like this? Had this all been just a fling to him, using Eddie for his body and caring nothing about him? Eddie recalled their last few weeks together, all the times they had shared, and wondered if they had all been a lie. He thought of how he had trusted Luke enough to let himself fall in love with him, how he had even given up his anal virginity to Luke, because he want-ed to, because he cared for him. Had even that been for a lie? He thought back to that moment, lying in Luke's chair, which Peter had lowered into a bed, his legs in the air, and the wondrous feeling of Luke's cock sliding inside of him, the connectedness he felt at that moment, when they were one. It had seemed so genuine, but perhaps it had all been an act, all Luke's intimacy and little gestures just a means to keeping him believing this was real, that they were in love with each other, when Luke was just doing it all for the opportunity to fuck him.

Eddie couldn't bear the thought and decided to let the tank run him over. But at the last moment, he dove to one side, cursing that the AI wasn't programmed to keep from running over their own men. What was the point of having a computer run the tank, if it can't tell who was the enemy and who wasn't?

And suddenly, Eddie realized what had happened. Luke had told Peter not to register him, not by voice, or image, or anything. Luke had no idea he was even there!

"Ha!" Eddie shouted, laughing. He picked up a rock and threw it at the retreating tank. Then, in a whisper, "You're just jealous, Peter, because he loves me." Smiling, Eddie returned to the barracks, dreaming about their reunion, a few weeks from then, when Luke would come back to him.

BRINGING ROGER HOME
by Giles Packer

When Roger moved in next door to me, I gave it no second thought. People come and go in the modern world, and I never pay that much attention to neighbors, unless they have loud, yapping dogs or lots of noisy, late night parties that I'm not invited to. But Roger was the friendliest guy I'd known since I was a kid. He always said 'hello', always had something to add, a question or a comment to make, and certainly never grunted his way by me in the halls the way most people in NY seem to do.

At first, I thought he must have been from out of town, probably some place like Nowhere, Nebraska, where everyone knew everyone and a crime wave describes what happens when a bunch of High School seniors go and knock down a few mailboxes with a baseball bat and a pickup truck. (I think I saw that in a movie once.) Then, when I realized that he didn't have anything but a pure city accent and that he had never made any comment to suggest that he was having some difficulty adjusting to big city life, I readjusted my thoughts and tried to figure out how the hell anyone could be so relentlessly cheerful.

As I got to know him, I could see that he didn't have much to be down about. He was only about 26 years old, healthy and good looking, with wavy, long hair and a neat square jaw that brought to mind images of cowboys - or Marlboro ads. He was working in advertising, just a few years out of college. And he had one hell of an active social life, coming in at all hours of the morning, sometimes alone, sometimes with an answering set of footsteps. He was a considerate neighbor - he and his guest would always be quite, and strain as I could, I never heard the sounds of coitus energetica coming from the other side of my wall.

I tried to do the same, keeping my lady friends on the quiet side, and my boyfriends in public places. I was a very compartmentalized man at the time. Women, I brought home. Men, I screwed with in baths, or sex clubs, or darkened back rooms. A few times, I'd done the nasty with some guys in the back of the trucks that park overnight in the meat packing district, and I dropped a load far too many times to count along the piers.

Don't ask me why I did this - I couldn't tell you. Once, when I was drunk and spilled all the details about my sex life out to a buddy, he said some tough shit about how I didn't think sex with guys was OK, so I did it away from where I was comfortable. I don't know, maybe he was right. I didn't think about it a lot. It was hard enough to get a little of both men and women without thinking of how I was doing it and what the implications were. I was just screwing around, that's all.

I ran into Roger in the laundry room one night. He said his usual happy hello, and I grunted and started pushing my wash into one of the big machines. Then, I thought better (I mean, the guy was only trying to be friendly!), so I said "Hi." back. I quickly added, "How're you doin'?"

"Real good," he shot back. "But you don't look too good yourself. Touch of the flu?"

In fact, I was just grumpy and achy, but it seemed like a convenient excuse for my slovenly appearance and antisocial temperament. I nodded.

"Poor guy. Listen. I got what'll make you feel better, if you want it."

Great, a drug dealer. "No thanks," I said.

"No, really. It's a special drink, a kind of lemon toddy. It's hot. It'll soothe your throat, and with a couple of aspirins to take care of the fever and head ache, you'll feel much better." He looked over at the dryer which had suddenly stopped, and got up to empty it. "I can give you the recipe if you want it, but I make it faster then you can, and I already have all the ingredients."

"OK, OK, you talked me into it," I said, surrendering. I figured a drink wouldn't do any harm, and if it got him to go away and leave me alone, it was worth the possibility that I would have to pour it down the sink.

"Great!" He dumped a pile of clothing out onto the folding table and started quickly sorting through it. "As soon as I get upstairs, I'll start it. You can leave your wash to spin for a while, right? I'll bring it by in no time."

"Thanks," I muttered. I emptied the little box of detergent into my washer, slipped the quarters into the slots and started it up. As I turned around to leave, I saw him folding up a garish pair of boxer shorts, I mean really tacky. They had a saying on them, which I couldn't see all of, but I knew the design. They probably said "Home of the Whopper". I couldn't help it, I started to laugh.

He sighed, and quickly folded them up small. "They're not mine," he said sheepishly.

"No, they just ended up in your laundry!"

"Let's say that they were accidentally left behind," he replied firmly. But I could see a little bit of red coming up his collar, which was cute as hell. The boxers vanished underneath other clothing as he became as silent as any other New Yorker caught in the laundry room. Maybe he was waiting for me to ask how the hell someone could leave a pair of tacky underwear at his house, and what that meant. It took me a few seconds to wonder about it, actually, and then I caught his eye.

Well, fuck me blind--he was into guys!

But here I was, at home, and not even in my good grungy clothes, and there was no way I was gonna start something with a guy who lived next door, for crying out loud. I shrugged and headed for the door.

"I'll bring that drink by in a few minutes," he called after me.

"OK," I called back, not looking. Listen, I told myself, if the guy wants to be friendly, maybe he can feed the cat when you go away. I thought that he might have designs on me, but to tell you the truth, I couldn't really believe that he wanted to start something when we both lived in the same building.

I took a mental inventory when I got back to my place. He was good looking, clean shaven and slim, but not skinny. His hair was smooth and thick, just the kind that's nice to grab or stroke. It was hard to tell whether or not he had a nice, defined body, but he didn't look hairy as far as his arms went--so far so good. He always looked a few steps out of the shower, neat and bright and disgustingly healthy.

I, on the other hand, was a bit of a mess. In my old sweats and bare feet, a worn t-shirt sagging over my shoulder, I must have cut one fine figure of a slob downstairs. I ran a hand through my hair, hoping that it would fall better when I stopped, but it didn't. I considered changing. And then I reminded myself that he was coming over to give me medicine.

Besides, I didn't want to get involved with someone who lived next door, remember?

It was all kind of strange for me. I kicked a few things out of the way and stuck some dirty dishes into the dishwasher to get the off my counter. The least I could do is not let him think I was a total slob.

He came by in about ten minutes, with a pitcher and a huge mug, the kind you'd get at a street fair, with swirly designs all over it.

"Sit down," he said at once. "Sit down, make yourself comfortable. You're going to love this, you'll see."

"Thanks," I started to say.

"Hey, no problem, neighbor." He looked around, and I pointed at the kitchen table, and he put the pitcher down. I took a seat and leaned my elbows on the table so I could take a whiff. It smelled like whisky and lemons, not bad.

"This is an old recipe, from my Grandma," he explained, pouring. I watched as his shirt tugged up at the waistband, exposing a bare, tanned lower back that looked smooth enough to lick. He kept going: "I made extra, so you can heat it up later if you want more. But you shouldn't have more then one in a four hour period. It'll get you smashed!"

"OK," I said, taking the mug. It was really hot, and I jerked my fingers away.

"Give it a little time," he cautioned. "Breathe in the steam, you'll like it."

Obediently, I did, and immediately, my mouth watered. It was like hot lemonade, with that heavy underscent of good whisky. I leaned back and savored it. Damn, if I did have the flu, that stuff would be heavenly. I looked over at Roger and tried a smile. He saw it and lit up like a Christmas angel, all teeth and sincerity.

"Good shit," I said.

He laughed. "Yeah, it is. While you're waiting for it to cool a little how about a backrub?"

"Oh, no, that's not nec-"

"Sure it is. It'll be just a minute!" He cracked his knuckles neatly and stepped behind me and lowered his soft hands to my shoulders.

"No, really man," I protested.

"You are stiff as a board," he complained, kneading into me. "When was the last time you had a massage?"

"I am being totally bullied," I complained, leaning back. "Stop. Ohhh. . . stop. . ."

"Sure thing, as soon as you're done," he said. His fingers worked their way past the iron plating around my neck, and started to unfasten all the pins and seams that made me into the tense wreck I was, and then the heat began to soak in. I sipped cautiously at the toddy and relaxed back into his probing hands.

"This is the most contrived seduction I've ever done," he said suddenly. "Is it working?"

I nearly spit out the toddy, but knowing what was good for me, I swallowed it first. "Jesus!" I cried out, turning my head. "That's fucking direct!"

"It seemed like the best way," he replied. He looked down at me and firmly turned my shoulders back into the position he needed. "I mean, the next step was to get you tipsy and then into bed. But I'd rather have you sober."

"How could you tell?" I asked, without the energy or desire to feel angry anymore. His fingers continued to work on my muscles.

"I don't know. You seemed like an OK guy. You're hot. And you don't say stupid things about fags and women." He stroked the back of my neck. "Mrs. Larabie, in 4A told me that you sometimes bring girls back, and also stay out all night."

The old biddy. See if I brought in her mail any more.

"And Frank - you know, over in 6F? He said he saw you down at the Pit one night."

"The Pit?" I almost jerked away from his still-working hands. A neighbor saw me at that dive? And recognized me?

"Yep. He said you were having quite a party with three or four banjee boys in bike pants and ripped t-shirts."

Oh. That would have been me, yes. All I remembered that night was the rich smell of so many men all over me, and the taste of their bodies, and the slick feel of the oil we had poured all over the place. One of them had a tattoo that said "Caliente", and he had lived up to that label. . .

"Outed by my neighbors," I offered lamely.

"Oh, please," he chuckled back. "It took me three weeks to get that much about you. In the mean time, I also found out that you used to be a carpenter, you have a cat, and you're not very friendly."

"Yet you wanted to pick me up anyway."

"I bring out the friendly side of people." With that sentiment worthy of a Hallmark card, he slipped his warm hands down the front of my shirt and caressed my chest. "Wanna see how?" he asked, tonguing my ear.

My first instinct was to say no - really! After all, I didn't want to carry on with someone - with a guy - in my own building. But his determined touches and the warmth of his body were too much. Also, I had never been so ardently pursued before in my life. It was a tremendous turn-on to be wanted that much. I took another deep drink of the toddy and leaned back so he could kiss me. The lemony whisky mix flowed over our lips and mingled between our tongues, and I knew that his mouth would be heavenly on my cock.

"I'm a mess," I said half-heartedly when we came up for air.

"I'll fix you up," he said with a chuckle. And with that, I left myself in his so-soft hands.

First, he pulled me out of my chair and propelled me into my own bedroom. "My, we're direct," I commented as I flopped onto the unmade bed.

"Shut up and take what's coming to you," he snapped. "Take your shirt off." I did, and he moved me around on the bed until I was laying across it on my stomach. He knelt over me, and began a real massage, working his way from my already-feeling-good shoulders down my back. He was fantastic! His skin was soft, but the strength behind his hands loosened me up in no time. I started to purr, just like a kitten, when his fingers worked their magic on my lower spine and started to trickle down the waistband of my sweats.

"Keep going," I muttered, lifting my hips up. He tugged the sweats down, and the slight breath of the air above my bare ass was deliciously teasing. My dick was already nice and hard from all the attention being paid to my body, but I was in no mood to hurry him up. I wanted to see what he would do next.

Roger pulled the sweats away from my legs and then settled back into massaging me, running his palms down my legs with every new stroke. Sometimes, he would scratch my skin with his fingernails, which also felt wonderful, and then he'd resume his long, slow manipulation of my muscles and flesh. It was heavenly.

When I was completely bare and feeling like a sultan, he turned me over, and started working his way back up my body. It's lovely to get massaged over the front of your body - he hit places that no one had ever gripped hard except during sex, like the front of my thighs. He avoided my groin, ignoring my bouncing, hard-as-a-rock dick, and gently massaged my stomach and then my chest.

"You planning to stay dressed?" I asked.

"Not for much longer", he said. "Just relax, you'll get everything you want."

"How do you know what I want?" I countered.

"I know", he assured me. And with that, he began to really work on my upper chest, digging his fingers into my pecs and gathering up skin under his hands. It felt fabulous, rough and sexy, and by the time he reached my nipples and started playing with them, I was thrusting my dick up at his thighs, trying to rub it against his sweet body. I groaned as his fingers expertly worked my nips to attention and then some.

"You know, you're sounding much worse," he whispered into my ear. "Maybe you need some more direct attention."

I had just started to nod when his lips crushed against mine, and his hot tongue began to thrust its way between my teeth. He kissed me like a girl, all softness covering wet action. I reached up and hugged him to me and began to tug his shirt off.

Nice bod, real nice. Tan and flexible and smooth, with a tight stomach, just the way I like it. I worked my hands down around his ass cheeks and got a good handful, pressing him hard against my groin.

He laughed and pulled up. "I know just what the patient needs," he said with a gleam in his eye. And I mean a real gleam! The kid was right out of a fantasy! He stood up and shucked off his pants, revealing a tight pair of hip-hugger briefs, electric blue, and left them on as he hunkered down and blew a mouthful of hot air against my cock.

"Come on, you fucking tease, suck me off!" I barked. I was already feeling dizzy!

"You got it," he said, and in one swoop of his soft lips, he covered my aching prick from knob to base, taking me all in like a fucking pro. I arched my back, pushing my dick up into the back of his throat, but he pulled away, slurping as he drew back.

"Oh no," he said, grasping my cock in one firm hand. "You're the patient. Just lie back and take your medicine."

Cursing him in the names of all the saints and angels, I dropped my ass back on the bed and let him continue the way he wanted to. Man, could he suck cock! His mouth seemed to be everywhere, pulling the skin around my balls, wrapping itself around the crown, lapping a hot tongue up and down my shaft like it was a giant piece of candy, he never paused to enjoy a single position or style. When his tongue lapped at my piss-hole, his hands were busy cupping my balls and jacking off my shaft.

"I'm gonna cum, I'm gonna cum!" I screamed out, when that pleasure became too overwhelming. And wouldn't you know, my sucking neighbor pulls back again, and laughs as he hears my groan of anguish.

"You act like you don't want this monster up my tight ass," he said, meeting my eyes. "Am I wrong? Should I keep going?"

"Shit!" I growled, fighting not to cum right there and then. Man, what a choice! More of that sweet cocksucking and ball licking, or slamming my boner into a new butt! How the fuck was I supposed to make that choice?

Luckily, he made it for me. "I guess you want to be sucked off - this time." He sighed, as if he was disappointed, but he looked happy as a pig in shit when he swooped down on my pecker again and slammed his face down to my balls.

Roger started to make sharp grunting noises as he throat-massaged my dick-head. Each contraction of his throat pulled and compressed my flesh, until I began to feel the onset of a superjetting cum, the kind that you think will hit the ceiling when your jerking off. I threw one arm back and grabbed the back of his head in my free hand, pressing him against my crotch as I began to thrust up into him again.

This time, he didn't pull away. He knew it was the right time. I growled and snarled as I jerked my dick into his face, feeling his hot spit pouring over my shaft and balls, his tongue never still, always working me, lapping at me, the point digging into my shaft like a finger working on my cum tubes.

"Oh, yeah!" I shouted, feeling the hot jazz begin to spurt. "Suck that down! Take it!"

And he did, every last drop, as I spasmed and shot his mouth full of my sizzling juice! And still he didn't stop! While I was relaxing my body back on the bed, he kept his mouth sealed over my tube, sucking up every drop of my cum, and licking around the edges of his lips to catch what might have dribbled out. And still he stayed, licking and gently cleaning off my shaft as it relaxed back too, until it was a normal unengorged size, and resting in a curve over my balls. (Which felt great, by the way!)

Then, and only then, did he gently disengage his mouth, just a second before I was gonna moan to let him know he was pushing it.

Perfect. Fucking perfect cocksucking. From my fucking neighbor.

I took deep breaths and barely knew it when he left the room. When he came back, he was a warm, damp washcloth.

"Gonna jerk me off again?" I joked.

"Shut up. You're the patient," he reminded me. And like some character out of a fucking book, he wiped me down with the cloth, cleaning my sweat (and his) off me. There wasn't a drop of cum to wipe away from my cock and balls, but he swiped at them anyway, until I did groan. As I relished the feel of the warmth and the following coolness, he flopped down next to me, his dick hard and long, like the rest of his body.

"The prognosis is good," he said with a grin. "I think you'll survive."

I looked at him, and back at his cock. He showed no signs of being angry or impatient, even though he had a boner that already dribbled precum and looked about hard enough to hammer nails.

"I think so too," I said. "But the doc doesn't seem to be in good shape."

"Don't knock it," he told me. "I try to hold on for a long time, so I have better control when I fuck."

"You fuck too?"

"The better to take care of my poor sick patients!"

Shit. A great cock-sucker like that, and a top as well, with a nice body and a cock to match, and an unbelievably cheerful disposition, and he lived in my fucking building.

"Hey, Rog," I said, pulling one arm under my head. "How's about dinner, tomorrow night?"

"Sure," he shrugged. "Got a favorite place to go?"

"I figure right here is about my favorite place right now."

He grinned and stretched out next to me, sighing as I grabbed hold of his dick. "Sounds real good to me," he said.

And you know what? It sounded pretty good to me, too.

FAXING OFF
by David Laurents

I forgot all about Jack Springer until I got an entry-level job, via a trick who'd turned into a friend, at one of those glossy entertainment and fashion magazines. I'd exchanged numbers with Jack at a bar, and only when I got home and went to write him up in my Little Black Book did I notice he'd written "fax only" next to the number he'd given me. I was pissed, and was ready to throw the matchbook cover with his info in the trash. I mean, it took a lot of nerve to presume that everyone in the world had a personal fax machine, or implied that he was only interested in the type of people who did. At the time I was waiting tables at a chic French restaurant uptown, so I didn't even have access to a fax at work. But I kept the number anyway. I keep very good records of the men I meet. If only the IRS would audit my Little Black Book instead of my taxes!

Anyway, when my new boss showed me the fax machine on my first day and was explaining where the extra reams of paper were kept and who to call for help if it jammed, I only paid half attention to her. Jack's distinguished profile had leapt into my mind, and I could hardly wait until I went back to my desk, where I could check my Little Black Book. A few weeks after I'd met him at Baxter's, the Sunday paper ran an interview with him in the magazine section. I had recognized the photo of him right away, and that was the image that came to mind as I was standing beside the fax machine. He wasn't all that handsome, really, at least, not drop-dead handsome. But he was distinguished. He'd aged well, and had an air of high culture about him, which is what had attracted my attention to him in the bar. He photographed well, and this high society air came across in the pictures they ran on him with the interview. I remembered how my estimation of him had soared a couple of notches when I saw the profile in the papers. I mean, he was practically famous! I had always meant to pick up one of his books when I was in a bookstore, but I just kept forgetting...

As soon as I could, I sat down at my new desk and checked my notes about him. "Nice Basket" I had written in the same color pen as the fax number, along with "Author" and "Baxter's". The interview had filled in most of the rest of the details, and made me forgive him for giving me a fax instead of phone number. He was a writer, novels mostly, and worked out of his home. That was why he didn't have a regular phone--too much of a distraction. People calling when he was trying to work. The temptation to call someone up and chat for an hour, or worse, make plans to do something during his working time was too strong for him. With the fax, he didn't need to read messages as they came in, letting them pile up until he had finished a chapter and was ready for a break. In this age of high technology, he could still take care of most of his business by fax instead of phone: his editor, many of his friends--even the Chinese food place down the block. He could fax an order over, and 15 minutes later they'd deliver it to his door.

I smiled, pleased that I still could remember so much about him from my notes and the interview I'd read. I wondered if he remembered me as well, and doubted it, which is why, though I still had his fax number, I waited for an excuse to contact him. I resolved to at last get one of his books when I went to lunch and read it that night, so I'd have an excuse to fax him tomorrow. I was excited about connecting with him again, even though there had never seemed to be much chance of our ever sleeping together. Part of my excitement, I think, was having someone to fax to; the novelty of that appealed to me. I hoped he hadn't changed his number in the six months since I'd met him. If he really didn't have a phone, which seemed likely from what the interview had said and the fact that he'd given me his fax number at the bar in the first place, then he would want to keep his number constant so his editors and friends could reach him. I moved the book's little red ribbon to his

page and put away my Little Black Book before someone noticed I was-
n't working.

I didn't get much work done, though. My desk was out in the hallway
in front of my boss' office, and also across from one of the executive's
doors. He'd had his door closed all morning, but just when I settled
down to dive into the work my boss had given me he opened it, and
there went my ability to keep my mind on my work. He was gorgeous!
The kind of blond who tanned with a healthy looking pink glow just
exuding from every pore of his body--and I imagined quite a lot of them,
undressing him in my mind as I watched him sitting behind his desk
talking on the phone. He noticed me looking in his direction and
flashed me a million dollar smile, blindingly white teeth in an attention-
getting grin. My cock was hard as a flagpole and straining against the
crotch of my pants as if it meant to burst through the fabric. I wondered
if anyone would notice if I unzipped my pants to give my cock some
breathing room, but decided against it. I mean, it was still my first day
on the job!

I didn't know what to do. I couldn't think about the work I'd been
given, couldn't think about anything but the guy in the office across from
me. I looked away from him, staring at my computer screen, but
instead of the terminal all I saw was that smile, his chiseled chest and
abs, his cock, hard and waiting for me, his muscled legs up in the air,
his pink asshole winking at me, inviting. I wondered if the corporate
men's room was busy right then, if I could take five minutes and go jerk
off before I creamed in my pants anyway and regretted it. I had to do
something to get him out of my mind or I would be fired in a few hours,
for not being able to work.

I stared across the hallway, trying to read his name off his now-open
door, and wished that my boss had done introductions to everyone in
the office. No, perhaps it was better that she hadn't, I thought, since I
would probably have embarrassed myself somehow upon meeting him.
But I had no idea what to call him, and wanted something for my mind
to pin down, so I could be done thinking about him and get down to

work. I was so turned on by him, I was sitting there fantasizing about his name! I was almost ashamed of myself; it wasn't like I hadn't gotten my rocks off in a few weeks or something. But this guy just really turned my head, and my cock, and I couldn't think about anything else.

I figured if maybe I could talk to someone about him, I would get it out of my system, and I could then get back to work. But I couldn't very well call someone up and say all the things I wanted to do to this guy if I was sitting at my desk; what if my boss came by to ask what was taking me so long on the letters I was supposed to type? And what if he overheard me himself? I didn't, of course, have any friends yet in the office, and frankly, I doubted anyone else in this corporate headquarters was even queer, someone who I could stand with at the water-cooler and whisper my fantasies. I looked at my Little Black Book, wondering who I would call if my boss was at lunch and the coast was clear, who I might call in order to have some quick and sweaty sex during my lunch break so I wasn't as distracted during the afternoon, and suddenly I realized what I might do. I would write my fantasies about The Exec (which is how I thought of him since I didn't know his name) and fax them to Jack. I didn't know if he'd remember me, and I had no real excuse for writing to him out of the blue, but it was only 10:37 a.m., and there was no way I would last all morning without telling someone about The Exec and clearing my head. (And my balls.) I'd simply burst.

I opened a new file on the word processor and began to write:

Dear Jack--

You probably don't remember me. We met at Baxter's bar a few months ago. It was the Friday before the Tribune ran that profile of you in the Magazine section. I really enjoyed reading more about you; it made me want to rush out and read all your books.

I'm writing you now because I just got a new job, where I've got access to a fax machine. Well, I'm really writing you now because I've got nowhere else to turn. See, there's this executive in the office across from my desk, and he's just drop-dead gorgeous. I can't think about anything else but vaulting over my desk and tearing his clothes from him, hungrily running my hands across his well-built, tanned body. He looks like one of those stereotypical California surfers, only hotter, and you know he's got a brain, to boot, because he's a Top Exec at the magazine I now work for! But he's got this body to die for, a body to kill for, a body I can't stop thinking about!

He's got large hands and I keep watching them, curled around the thick earpiece of the phone. I can't hear what he's saying, but I imagine those big hands fisting his own thick cock.

I've never been so turned on by someone before, just from looking at them. I mean, I can get turned on by a lot of things, and even by men who you wouldn't ordinarily think of as attractive, but something in the way the carry themselves, or their mannerisms can do it for me. I don't know what it is about him that hits me so strong, though. It's as if he exudes this masculine sexuality in his every movement. He's probably straight, but that doesn't stop me from fantasizing! It almost makes it even better. I can imagine him fucking me like I was a woman, plowing into me in a workman-like fashion with his huge cock, his large nipples staring down at me from his chiseled torso.

And the idea of fucking him up the ass, that virgin straight ass, makes me so hard I feel I'm about to burst a new fly in these pants, and there goes my best work suit.

It's driving me crazy!

Hope you don't mind my having written to you like this. I had to tell somebody and my boss would've heard me if I called someone. You were the only person I knew with a fax who might understand. But don't write back to me, or I'll get in trouble. Fired my first day at the job for faxing off on the company machine!

Thanks for being a friendly ear. Will try and contact you again when I can be faxed back.

Gotta run.

--Eric

I printed it out and read it over again. Not wonderful prose--and Jack was a writer, so he'd care about things like that--but it would have to do. I started to get up to bring it over to the fax machine and send it to Jack, when I realized my erection was still poking up against the thin fabric of my slacks. I wondered if I should sit back until it went away, but then I looked up and saw The Exec standing behind the desk in his office, pacing as he talked on the phone, and I knew my erection wasn't going anywhere. My mind just couldn't seem to imagine this guy in clothes and kept erasing them. I stood and walked to the fax machine, casually holding a folder in front of me, feeling like I was back in high school hiding an erection behind my school books. I felt sure that everyone could tell what I was doing, and stuck one hand into my pocket to hide the bulge. I grabbed hold of my cock, ran my fingers along its throbbing, swollen length, and wished I could just go into The Exec's office, lock the door behind me and fuck until quitting time.

I was all sweaty nervous as I punched Jack's fax number into the machine. Mostly, it was from The Exec, of course, but there was this strange techno-thrill from illicitly using the fax machine like this. Jack's number was for some reason busy, and I wanted to swear at the machine as I waited for it to redial and connect. The longer I stood there, looking guilty and trying to hide my erection, the easier it would be for me to be caught. I tried to look nonchalant, as if I was just faxing something mundane for my boss, and carefully looked everywhere but at the fax machine.

Suddenly, I heard my name called out, and I looked up, startled and guilty. How could my boss have known? She stood at the door of her office, beckoning to me. I looked quickly at the fax machine, planning to grab my letter to Jack and hide it in my folders, to send later, but just then the machine connected, and the sheet of paper began its slow route through the insides of the fax machine. There was no way I could pull it out now, not without tearing it, and I couldn't leave my boss waiting there without her asking what I was doing. Nervous as hell that someone would get to the machine and read it before I had a chance to rush back and get the letter, I walked down the hallway, trying to put on a calm and collected air, as if the world was just peachy keen instead of hanging on the blade of a knife at my throat.

My boss wanted to show me some new trick on my computer. She made me sit down at my desk and stood over my shoulder, giving me directions. I wanted to rush back to the machine, certain that my fax had at last gone through and was just sitting there, waiting for someone to discover it, but I couldn't do anything. I had to sit there, with her leaning over me, the smell of her expensive flowery perfume making me sick, her small breast brushing against my shoulder every now and then and only reminding me of the totally hot Exec just across the way. I had to forcibly keep my eyes on the screen each time I felt her breast against my shoulder, lest I instinctively look at The Exec, but still my eyes saw him--his bare chest, his naked body lying before me, so inviting, the slight curve I imagined his cock held. I wondered if my boss had noticed my erection poking up in my lap, and if she did if she thought it was because of her. I tried to lean slightly forward and hide it. And all I could do was smile and nod and "a-hmm" at her directions. She left me to finish the file on my own, going back into her office but leaving the door open in case I needed more help. I was supposed to finish it right then, and to bring it to her when I was done. I raced through it, trying to make the most of my 65 wpm typing skills I'd picked up typing other kids' papers for money in college.

Suddenly, The Exec was standing in front of me! I couldn't help getting an eyeful of his large basket, which was at my eye level, just past the piece of paper he was holding out to me. I tore my eyes away from his crotch and looked up at his face. God, he was beautiful!

"I think this is yours," he said, and I almost died right there. Of all people to find the transmission I'd left in the fax machine, it had to have been The Exec! I knew he'd read it, how could he not? What must he think of me? I was going to get canned, I felt certain.

"Come into my office."

This was it, I thought as I followed behind him. I'd lasted under three hours at my new job... I couldn't help staring at his ass I trailed after him, though, and imagining working that tight bubble-butt.

The door shut firmly. He stood facing the window, motionless, except for the whir of his fingers drumming against the sill. I waited for him to turn around and fire me, his indignation, his rage. He turned to face me and I closed my eyes, bracing against the shock. I was a wimp. I just couldn't stand there and take it like a man, not knowing what he must think about me after reading that fax. I felt like a prisoner about to be executed, who asks for the blindfold, so he doesn't have to see the gunmen shooting him down.

He didn't say anything.

I waited.

I opened my eyes again, confused, and curious. He stood before me like an imposing blond monolith, silent and immovable. His face was placid and calm, his arms folded across his chest. My eyes continued downwards. His fly was unzipped and his cock thrust boldly from beneath the fabric, swollen and pink. My breath caught in my throat.

I sank to my knees before him, inwardly giving thanks to every deity I could remember. From this vantage I got a chance to examine in his thick cock in every detail, from the tiny little piss-hole on the tip of his fat glans to the blond hairs that curled around its base, still lost in the fabric of his pants. I'd been right about the slight curve, but wrong about which direction it bent. The vein that ran along the top throbbed as if with impatience, and I leaned forward to take him into my mouth. I flicked my tongue around the swollen crown, stretching my lips further and further as I took more of him into my mouth. I paused, working up saliva to smooth the way. Slowly, my lips slid closer and closer to his crotch, where the fly of his pants loomed like a dark cave.

I reached up and pulled his nuts from his clothes, massaging their hefty weight in my palm as I gulped down his cock.

My jaw ached. He grabbed my head and started pumping into my mouth, fucking my face in short quick thrusts. I started to gag as his cock pushed into the back of my throat, but I fought the rising bile and settled back on my knees, bracing myself until I was able to accommodate him.

Now that my hands were free, I unzipped my own pants and reached past my damp jockeys to free my own aching cock. I slicked the head with my own precum, and began whacking off in sync with his thrusting into my face. I'd been so worked up all morning that it wasn't long before my nuts let loose, and I was shooting thick ropes of cum between his legs onto the dark carpet. He didn't stop fucking my face, pumping his huge piece of meat into my mouth with the same even thrusting as before. My jaws had gone beyond aching and were numb, as he battered the back of my throat.

Suddenly he pulled out. A thread of spittle strung between my mouth and the tip of his cock.

"Suck on my nuts," he commanded, as his thick fingers curled about his meat and he began to fist himself as I'd imagined earlier. I eagerly dove into the dark, musky region between his legs and began sucking on his big balls, which were pulling up into his crotch as he got ready to cum. I slobbered from one to the other, getting them both wet, then trying to engulf both of them at once.

Suddenly, both of his balls popped out of my mouth at once and above me he roared. I sent my tongue flicking across the underside of his balls as he bucked forward above me. When he'd stilled, I stood up

David Laurents

and zipped myself up. He still hadn't really said anything to me. But as I waited, he merely pulled slowly on his still-swollen cock, lost in a pleasant post-coital haze.

Puddles of cum pooled on the blotter of his desk. I gathered this meant I wasn't about to be fired and, relieved, I began heading for the door, ready to get back to work before my boss got upset.

"Where do you think you're going?"

I looked back, surprised, then smiled. The Exec--I still didn't know his name!--had taken off his shirt, to reveal a torso even more exquisitely sculpted than I'd imagined. A small silver ring glinted in his left nipple. With one hand, he twisted his right nipple, while his other hand drifted across his wash-board stomach with its trail of downy blond hairs pointing towards his crotch.

I turned away from the door, thinking I'd have to write another fax to Jack Springer, thanking him for being there to listen to my fantasies and telling him the incredible things that had happened as a result.

About the Contributors

Barry Alexander, who lives in a small town in Iowa, is author of a collection of erotic stories ALL THE RIGHT PLACES (Badboy) and has published stories in the magazines IN TOUCH, INDULGE, BLACK MALE, ADVOCATE MEN, HONCHO, PLAYGUY, MANDATE, INCHES, HOT SHOTS, DRUMMER, and DADDY, among others, as well as in the anthologies HARD AT WORK, THE YOUNG AND THE HUNG, FRICTION 2, and others.

Tom Caffrey is the author of two collections of gay erotica, HITTING HOME & OTHER STORIES and TALES FROM THE MEN'S ROOM (both Badboy). His work has appeared in numerous magazines, as well as in the anthologies THE MAMMOTH BOOK OF GAY EROTICA, THE YOUNG AND THE HUNG, FLESH AND THE WORD 3, BEST AMERICAN EROTICA 1995, WANDERLUST, and FLASHPOINT.

Jameson Currier is the author of the novel WHERE THE RAINBOW ENDS and the story collection DANCING ON THE MOON. His short stories have appeared in many anthologies, including THE MAMMOTH BOOK OF GAY EROTICA, STOCKING STUFFERS, MEN ON MEN 5, BEST GAY EROTICA 1996, 1997, and 1998, THE MAN OF MY DREAMS, and others. He regularly contributes essays, articles, and reviews to many perdiodicals across the country, and is currently working as an associate editor for the NEW YORK BLADE.

Dominic Santi is a Los Angeles-based freelance writer whose stories have appeared in numerous anthologies--including HARD AT WORK, THE YOUNG AND THE HUNG, SEX TOY TALES, THE EROTIC WEB: THREADS FROM THE INTERNET, and THE MAMMOTH BOOK OF HISTORICAL EROTICA--as well as in various magazines, including ADVOCATE MEN, IN TOUCH, FIRSTHAND, and PENTHOUSE VARIATIONS. Santi is also section leader for Alternative Eros in CompuServe's Erotica forum.

Michael Lassell is the award-winning author of a colelction of (mostly erotic) stories, CERTAIN ECSTASIES (Painted Leaf Press); three collections of poetry, A FLAME FOR THE TOUCH THAT MATTERS (Painted Leaf), DECADE DANCE, and POEMS FOR LOST AND UNLOST BOYS; and a collection of essays, stories, and poems, THE HARD WAY (Richard Kasak Books). He is also the editor of the anthologies MEN SEEKING MEN: ADVENTURES IN GAY PERSONALS (Painted Leaf) and, with Lawrence Schimel, TWO HEARTS DESIRE: GAY COUPLES ON THEIR LOVE (St. Martin's Press), as well as two gay poetry anthologies, THE NAME OF LOVE (St. Martin's Press) and EROS IN BOYSTOWN (Crown). His writing has appeared in many anthologies, including AROUSED, THE MAMMOTH BOOK OF GAY EROTICA, THE BADBOY BOOK OF EROTIC POETRY, MEN ON MEN 3, and both the BEST GAY EROTICA and FLESH AND THE WORD series, as well as in numerous periodicals. He lives in New York City, where he works as an editor for METROPOLITAN HOMES magazine.

Chris Leslie is the publisher of DIRTY magazine, which can be found on the web at http://www.banjee.com/ His work has also appeared in various periodicals and anthologies, including THE MAMMOTH BOOK OF GAY EROTICA, STALLIONS AND OTHER STUDS, S/X, and THE EVERARD REVIEW, among others. He makes a living as a graphic designer in New York City.

Gilles Packer lives in Astoria, Queens, works in advertising, and has contributed erotic stories to numerous magazines.

Lawrence Schimel is an award-winning author and anthologist whose books include THE MAMMOTH BOOK OF GAY EROTICA (Robinson), THE DRAG QUEEN OF ELFLAND (Circlet Press), SWITCH HITTERS: LESBIANS WRITE GAY MALE EROTICA AND GAY MEN WRITE LESBIAN EROTICA (with Carol Queen; Cleis Press), PoMoSEXUALS: CHALLENGING ASSUMPTIONS ABOUT GENDER AND SEXUALITY (with Carol Queen; Cleis Press), and TWO HEARTS DESIRE: GAY COUPLES ON THEIR LOVE (with Michael Lassell; St. Martin's Press), among others. His work is included in more than 160 anthologies, such as BEST GAY EROTICA 97 and 98, THE RANDOM HOUSE BOOK OF SCIENCE FICTION STORIES, THE RANDOM HOUSE TREASURY OF LIGHT VERSE, GAY LOVE POETRY, SHAKESPEAREAN DETECTIVES, and THE MAMMOTH BOOK OF FAIRY TALES, among many others. Occasionally, he also writes for periodicals, and he has contributed to publications as diverse as THE SATURDAY EVENING POST, PHYSICS TODAY, and DRUMMER. He divides his time between his native New York and Madrid.

Walter Wilde is a freelancer writer and college professor who lives in Detroit.

About the Editor

David Laurents is the editor of the anthologies The Badboy Book of Erotic Poetry, Wanderlust: Homoerotic Tales of Travel, Southern Comfort, The Young and the Hung, and Hard at Work. His erotic short stories and poems have been published in many magazines, including Drummer, Torso, Mandate, First Hand, and Gay Scotland, as well as in various anthologies, including FLASHPOINT, SPORTSMEN, MY THREE BOYS, MAD ABOUT THE BOYS, PLAY HARD, and others. He lives in New York.

Acknowledgments

"After Hours" (c) 1999 by Chris Leslie. Reprinted by permission of the author.

"Nine Lives" (c) 1998 by Dominic Santi. Reprinted by permission of the author.

"Leash Broke" (c) 1998 by Barry Alexander. First published in INDULGE #28, January 1998. Reprinted by permission of the author.

"Spanish Summer" (c) 1997 by Lawrence Schimel. Reprinted by permission of the author.

"Yoshi, Honolulu, and the New Tattoo" (c) 1999 by Michael Lassell. Reprinted by permission of the author.

"Remembering" (c) 1995 by Tom Caffrey. Reprinted by permission of the author.

"Don't Ask, Don't Tell" (c) 1994 by David Laurents. First published in S/X. Reprinted by permission of the author.

"For the Record" (c) 1998 by Jameson Currier. First published in MASQUER-ADE NEWS LETTER. Reprinted by permission of the author.

"Kissing Cousins" (c) 1999 by Walter Wilde. Reprinted by permission of the author.

"Off the Menu" (c) 1998 by Barry Alexander. Reprinted by permission of the author.

"Bringing Roger Home" (c) 1996 by Gilles Packer. Reprinted by permission of the author.

"Faxing Off" (C) 1996 by David Laurents. First published in TORSO, March 1996. Reprinted by permission of the author.

College Days   EV16
Strip trivial pursuit, naked twister, raunchy, after-hours sex parties plus a hunky lecturer feature in this erotic tale of sexual innocence lost. With six English cuties.

Gym Babes   JE3
Keeping fit is always a priority for these Hungarian guys. However with all that gymnastics they need a little release. Working up a sweat they release their sexual tension away from prying eyes, in the changing room and in the showers.

The Castle   JE10
In search of their annual orgy, the guards of Castle Gay, two horny ghosts from the past come across two sexy young campers to seduce. Needing to satisfy their sex drives they soon find more willing victims to satiate their desires.

hotXXXvideos

Tender Young Lust
EV13

A Liverpool ferry trip ends in a steamy romance when 19 year old Julian gets to grips with slim blond Tim in his new underwear. Sparks fly when cute Anthony and a sexy horseback rider get left alone. PJ the 21 year old footballer gets aroused as he flicks through a EuroGuy.

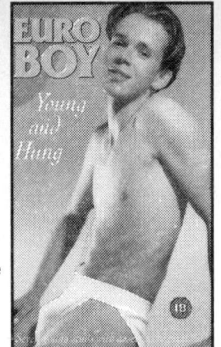

Young And Hung
EV14

Seven sexy young lads with perfect slim bodies, pert buns and sizeable assets star in this hour long sexcapade. Watch them cool down as they strip down and frolic in the pool.Spying on each other's naked bodies they soon get aroused and horny.

London Lovers 2
EV17

Nine fresh faces and 90 minutes of raunchy sexscenes. City slickers in a lunch time cop-off, two lovers devour each other over dessert and a nineteen year old marine in a steamy shower jerk off.

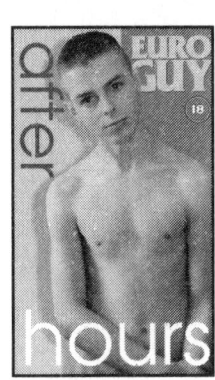

After Hours
EV18

Six well-hung cuties are caught on camera as they have fun after hours in Prowler Soho. Ever ready to mix business with pleasure, the assistants get raunchy in the stockroom, flirt with the customers changing in the fitting room and punish horny shop-lifters.

Water Babes   JE4

The swim team are training hard for the Hungarian finals but the sight of each other in tight swimming costumes soon turns these horny boys on. In between training they leave nothing unexplored as they sneak off for gay passion.

Ski School   JE6

At an Austrian ski resort, seven gorgeous athletes relax and unwind between gruelling sessions on the slopes. Steamy clinches, raunchy sex sessions and laddish outdoor pursuits soon have these guys fulfilling their sexual appetites.

THE HARDLINE
MAN 2 MAN
Credit Card Line
0171 915 6100
CRUISELINE
MAIL BOX
FANTASIES
CONFESSIONS
0839 400 370
calls cost 50p per minute
WEB COMMUNICATIONS. PO BOX 2041 RH20 1YB

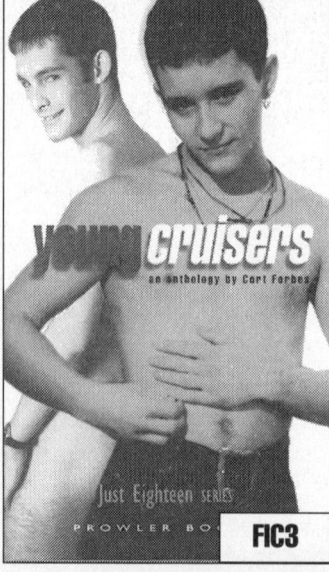

Young Cruisers FIC3 £5.99

The third novel to cum out of the Just Eighteen series is a tantalising selection of short stories on sleazy first time adventures. Black and Blue is a passionate story of how a young guy gets fucked for the first time by his fantasy man, a stud with a giant cock. Been There, Done That takes us into the world of hustlers where Ty unsatisfied with his tricks goes out and gets his fair share of hot spunky action.

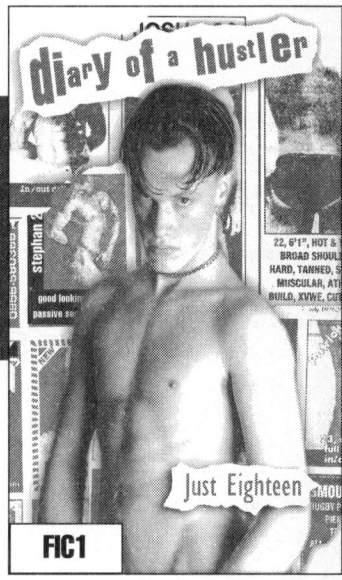

Slaves FIC2 £5.99

Slaves is the tale of Jack's sexual encounters which begin as he joins the mile high club. Cumming off the plane he falls headlong into one horny sexploit after another. Under cover as a journalist writing about the slave trade, Jack gets more than his fair share of native cock.

Diary Of A Hustler FIC1 £5.99

Follow the escapades of 18 year old Joey as he goes through his hot'n'horny training for his first hustling jobs. As muscular Thane shows Joey the ropes they soon realise that Joey's young blond boyish looks will be popular with a host of men looking for that ideal plaything.

Corporal In Charge FIC4 £5.99

Twenty short stories of hot and sleazy sex. Fritscher details each story down to the last drop of cum. From teenage wank sessions to college locker room fun to hard sex in the army, this book covers every fantasy.

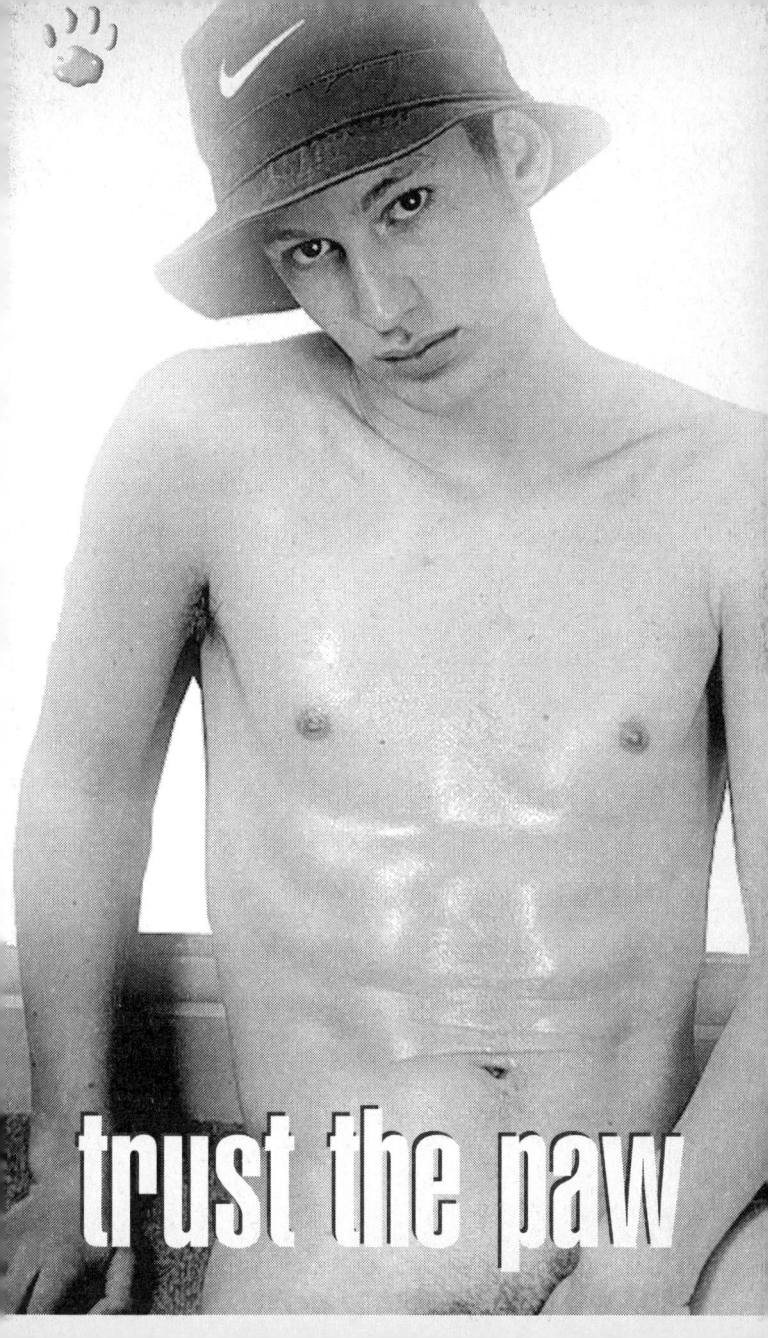

prowler magazine subscriptions

EuroGuy Mag 108   EG108

Featuring hot 18-21 year olds who's cute and fresh young faces will get you horny in no time. One smooth, tanned boy-next-door tells you about his first threesome where they took it in turns to take from behind while our gorgeous young Hung-arian pictured on the right gets up to mischief in the open-air. With another 8 pages of stiff, throbbing cocks, you'll love this issue of EuroGuy.

Real Men Mag 3   RM3

Muscular men with cum-to-bed-eyes and rippling muscles ready to burst out. With more pecs, abs and bulging thighs than ever. Also included is the story of a man who fucks his way around the world in 80 lays and a steamy guide backrooms. Don't forget your 8-page hard section of horny suck'n'fuck action from the best of the latest US hardcore films.

Spunky Mag 7   SP7

Young, fresh and daring you to look, Spunky has a better than ever fill of gorgeous guys who wanna get naked with you. Take in our special features like the raunchy photo stories and readers' pics in sexpose. Don't forget your special eight page stiff bit where these sexy boy-men show off their hard love-muscles.

Other books in the PROWLER BOOKS collection:

Fiction:
Diary of a Hustler
- ISBN 0-9524647-64
Slaves
- ISBN 0-9524647-99
Young Cruisers
- ISBN 0-9524647-72
Corporal in Charge
- ISBN 0-95246478-0
Hard
- ISBN 0-902644-01-8
Active Service
- ISBN 0-902644-06-9
the Young and the Hung
- ISBN 0-902644-07-7
Aroused
- ISBN 0-902644-08-5
Brad
- ISBN 0-902644-09-3
Summer Sweat
- ISBN 0-902644-10-7
Campus Confessions
- ISBN 0-902644-11-5
Going Down
- ISBN 0-902644-12-3

Photographic:
Planet Boys
- ISBN 0-9524647-13
Kama Sutra of Gay Sex
- ISBN 0-9524647-05

Travel:
New York Scene Guide
- ISBN 1-90264400-X
Paris Scene Guide
- ISBN 1-902644-02-6